"Have you a _____ **a skeptic? O**_____ **at nervous?"**

"Come on," Eric said. "You waltz into my life with some crazy story about a sister I never knew I had? Wouldn't you have some doubts, too? A desperate woman looking to find a decent home for her baby can come up with a very convincing lie."

She leveled him a look that would have made most men back off in a hurry. "I personally guarantee that if you don't want to raise the girls for any reason at all, they will always have a good home—with me."

The intensity of her words brought him up short. This woman was not fooling around. "You want to adopt the twins?"

"With all my heart." A fine sheen of tears appeared in her eyes, but she didn't let them spill over.

"Then why did you bother to track me down? I never would have known otherwise."

"Because I promised I would."

ABOUT THE AUTHOR

Charlotte Maclay can't resist a happy ending. That's why she's had such fun writing more than twenty titles for Harlequin American Romance, Duets and Love & Laughter, plus several Silhouette Romance books. Charlotte is particularly well-known for her volunteer efforts in her hometown of Torrance, California; her philosophy is that you should make a difference in your community. She and her husband have two married daughters and four grandchildren, whom they are occasionally allowed to baby-sit. She loves to hear from readers and can be reached at P.O. Box 505, Torrance, CA 90508.

Books by Charlotte Maclay

HARLEQUIN AMERICAN ROMANCE

Don't miss any of our special offers. Write to us at the following address for information on our newest releases.

Harlequin Reader Service
U.S.: 3010 Walden Ave., P.O. Box 1325, Buffalo, NY 14269
Canadian: P.O. Box 609, Fort Erie, Ont. L2A 5X3

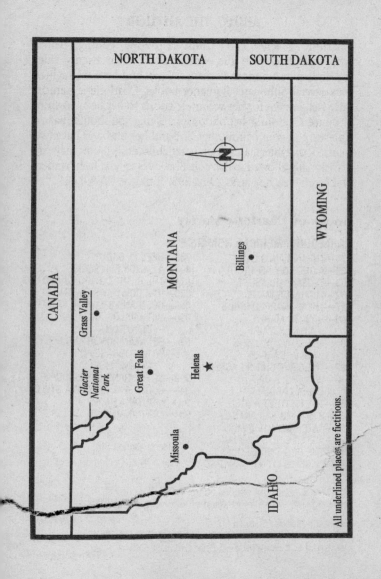

NORTH DAKOTA

SOUTH DAKOTA

CANADA

WYOMING

MONTANA

Grass Valley

Billings

Glacier National Park

Great Falls

Helena

Missoula

IDAHO

All underlined places are fictitious.

Chapter One

"I'm going to be a father."

Still stunned by the news, Sheriff Eric Oakes sat down heavily in the swivel chair behind his desk, trying to figure out how it had happened. Or if it could possibly be true.

His brother Rory, who had just come into the office, looked at him as if he'd lost his mind. "You're kidding."

"Twins. Girls."

"Hey, I didn't even know you were seeing anyone. How come you're keeping secrets from—"

"No, it's not like that. It's like—" He was stammering almost as much as the woman who'd called him with the news a few minutes ago. "They're my sister's kids." Three months old, the woman had said.

Rory frowned, and a hank of his dark hair slid across his forehead. In a futile gesture, he shoved it back into place. "Have you been nipping at that bottle you keep in your bottom desk drawer? You don't have a sister. Two brothers, me and Walker. Unless ol' Sharpy has had a sex change I don't know about—''

"No, that's not it." Eric pushed back from his desk, stood and paced across the room to look out the window onto the town of Grass Valley, Montana, located not far from the Canadian border.

Small was the only way to describe the town.

Rory's veterinary clinic was down a side road a block away, across from Doc Justine's medical clinic where Rory's bride, Kristi, worked as a nurse practitioner, helping her grandmother, the long-time town doctor.

On the main street there was a garage with rusty old heaps parked around it, a drugstore that sold more ice cream than prescriptions, and a general store. The saloon with a tattered banner that announced "Good Eats" was the only place that ever drew a crowd, except for the nearby church.

Crime wasn't a big issue in the community. A few Saturday-night drunks to fill his two jail cells now and then. Traffic accidents on the highway that called for him to respond. Occasional reports of cattle rustling or adolescent vandalism. A safe place to live.

And to raise kids, he thought as a lump formed in his throat. He'd always wanted children. A family of his own.

He turned back to his brother. "Some woman called a couple of minutes ago, a Laura somebody from Helena. She says my mother had another baby after she abandoned me." It was no big deal to tell Rory he'd been dumped by his mom. Rory's mother had done the same thing to him. That's how they'd both ended up at the Double O Ranch as foster kids to Oliver Oakes, who'd eventually adopted them and another kid, their brother, Walker—nicknamed Sharpy because he'd once shot himself in the leg. Walker was running the ranch nowadays.

"According to this woman, my sister's name was Amy Thorne, and she had twins a couple of months ago. Then she died." Still incredulous about the phone call, he shook his head. "She wanted me to have the babies. Be their dad. Apparently I'm their only living relative."

"Somebody's putting you on."

"I don't know. This Laura person sounded pretty legit." Except she'd been nervous, stuttering and stammering as she tried to tell her story.

"No, it's got to be some kind of scam. Did she ask for money? Child support?" Rory hooked his hip over the corner of Eric's desk and crossed his arms. His Native American heritage sometimes gave him a brooding look, but since discovering that he had a son and his recent marriage to the boy's mother, Kristi Kerrigan, Rory had been all smiles. Until now.

"The whole phone call kind of caught me off guard," Eric said. He was still shaken, half disbelieving the news yet wanting it to be true. "But no, she didn't say anything about money." Not that he could remember, at any rate. "She's going to bring the twins up here tomorrow."

"And just hand them off to you?"

"I don't know. She said something about interviewing me.'' Which didn't make a whole lot of sense. Either he was the twins' uncle or he wasn't. And if he wasn't, that woman wouldn't have bothered to call and make him identify himself by his birth name, Eric Johnson. A name he hadn't used since he was fifteen and Oliver Oakes adopted him. Eric had celebrated his thirty-second birthday last fall out at the ranch. Walker's wife, Lizzie, had baked the most lopsided cake he'd ever seen—not that he or anyone else had cared. Devil's food with chocolate frosting was hard to beat whatever the shape.

He shoved his fingers through his hair, shorter than Rory's, more brown than black and several shades lighter. Now that he was trying to explain this baby situation to his brother, it sounded pretty damn crazy. Maybe it was a hoax. One of those adolescent games when a kid calls someone and asks if their refrigerator is running. When the victim says yes, the kids giggle and say you'd better catch it before it runs out the door. A silly, harmless prank.

But his caller hadn't sounded like a kid. More like a woman with a sultry voice who hadn't wanted to call him at all.

And the story of his mother, who had run through boyfriends like water through a sieve, sounded legit, too. She could have gotten pregnant again.

God, could it be that all these years he'd had a sister who he didn't even know existed and now she was dead? He'd never have a chance to meet her. Or talk to her. Why hadn't she come looking for him sooner?

Or could that call have been nothing more than a cruel trick? The woman the same kind of person who would abandon her own kid?

Tears stung at the backs of his eyes as memories assailed him. He'd been ten years old and standing in the parking lot of a fast-food hamburger joint. Looking for his mother and her current boyfriend. Looking for their car. He knew where it had been parked. It wasn't there anymore. He'd had to go to the john. They'd left without him. God, he'd felt so alone. So hurt.

How could any mother do that to a kid?

He hadn't had a sister then. He'd been an only child, crowded into the back seat of the car along with everything they owned, and making it a point to stay out of reach of his mom's boyfriend. The guy had big meaty fists, Eric remembered that. And he knew how to use them.

A sob rose in his throat.

The office door opened to admit a current of fresh spring air along with Rory's wife, Kristi, and their son, Adam.

Swiping the back of his hand across his face, Eric struggled to pull his emotions back under control.

"Hi, Uncle Eric." The dark-haired five-year-old made a beeline for the nearest jail cell and began to swing on the door, peering out through the bars.

"Where did I put that key?" he asked, playing the game he and the boy had started recently. "I've caught me a monkey and I need to lock him up."

The youngster giggled and made scratching gestures under his arm pits. "Hoot-hoot-hoot."

Kristi stood on tiptoe to brush a kiss to her husband's cheek. "Ted Pomperan is at the clinic with a dog that cut its foot."

"Okay, I'll be right there. Eric's been telling me he's going to be a daddy. Twins, he says."

"Girls," Eric added. If the tale was true.

"You're kidding!" Kristi whirled toward him, her eyes widening. "I certainly hope you plan to marry the woman."

"Well, no. I mean, I don't even know the woman. She just called a couple of minutes—"

"I'd say you know her plenty well enough if she's going to have your babies," Kristi insisted.

Adam piped up. "Does that mean I'm gonna get some more cousins?"

"She's *not* going to have my babies. They're already three months old. And they might not even be—"

"So she hadn't told you she was—"

"Rory!" Eric came around the desk, caught Rory and Kristi by their respective elbows, ushering them toward the door. "Go take care of your canine patient, and in the meantime will you please explain the situation to your wife so she doesn't think I've committed some mortal sin."

"I'm not sure I get the picture myself," Rory complained.

"Neither do I. With luck, when the woman shows up tomorrow with the twins, I'll be able to figure out what's going on." *Assuming she comes at all.*

Rory opened the door for his wife.

"You be nice to the woman, Eric Oakes," Kristi admonished him. "If she's had your babies, she'll be feeling very vulnerable and unsure of herself. I know that's how I felt when I came back to Grass Valley and had to face Rory and tell him about Adam."

Exasperated, Eric said, "Talk to her, bro." He eased them out the door, closing it behind them and drew a deep breath.

Incredible. Was he really about to become a father of two baby girls?

Which reminded him that he didn't know squat about babies and diapers and bottles or any of that stuff. How the hell was he going to manage if it came to that?

Turning around, his gaze landed on Adam, who was still behind bars.

"Your folks just left."

The boy lifted his shoulders in an easy shrug. "The door locked itself. I can't get out."

"Right." He headed for the ring of keys hanging on a peg behind his desk.

Not only did he know little about caring for babies, he wasn't all that sure he'd be able to handle a couple of girls Adam's age when the time came. And God help him, when they became adolescents, his goose would be cooked.

If they were his nieces and he was about to become their daddy.

"I DON'T KNOW how you can give away those sweet little babies." Barbara Cavendish shaded her eyes against the morning sun as Laura loaded the twins inside her SUV for the trip to Grass Valley.

"It's what their mother wanted. Amy made that abundantly clear." A knot formed in Laura's throat at the mere thought of handing the twins over to a perfect stranger, even if he was their only living relative. And she fully understood that in her mother's heart, she'd already claimed the twins as her grandchildren.

Laura tried for a brave smile as she adjusted Amanda's car seat, then reached across her to the second car seat and caressed the blond fuzz on Rebecca's head. She'd never seen two more beautiful babies, small for their age but absolutely perfect in every way. She desperately hoped that once their uncle Eric met the twins he wouldn't feel the same way about them as she did. There was no law that said he *had* to raise them. He could easily reject the idea once he realized what it entailed.

"You know I loved Amy as if she were my own child," her mother continued. Barbara Cavendish had taken Amy into her home and heart as an abused foster child when the girl had been only ten years old. Laura had become her big sister—a role she'd loved and continued as best she could after Amy had moved out on her own. "I'm just not sure she was thinking clearly, wanting to give her babies away to a complete stranger when she knew you—''

''Her half brother, Mom.''

''Who she didn't even know existed until she rummaged through that shoe box of things her mother left her. I wish you hadn't hired that private detective to find the man.''

In more ways than Laura could count, she wished that too. ''I promised Amy I'd follow her wishes if I could.''

During Amy's last trimester of pregnancy, it had become clear she wouldn't be able to continue working as a waitress, and the complications of Amy's diabetes made the pregnancy high risk. She was told she could die.

Not wanting to burden Laura's mother, who tended to be overly protective, Amy had moved in with Laura. Soon after that she'd discovered she had a half brother—the twins' only living blood relative.

Then the worst had happened. Amy slipped into a coma before she gave birth to the twins. Only the doctor's quick action, taking the babies by cesarean section, had saved them. Amy had given her life for the children she never had a chance to hold.

Preparing for that contingency, she'd left written instructions for Laura to follow, signed and notarized, as binding as any will. Find Amy's half brother, if she could. See if he'd be a suitable daddy. If not, Amy wanted Laura to raise her babies. In the end, the decision would be Laura's.

It had taken the private detective three months and

several thousand dollars to locate the man. Five hours from now, give or take a little, Laura would actually meet him.

"In spite of the rocky road she'd traveled, Amy believed families ought to stick together," Laura told her mother. "I suspect you were the one who taught her that."

"I don't know, dear—"

"Mom, I have to do this. I gave my word of honor." Straightening, she rested her hand lightly on her mother's shoulder, trying to reassure herself as much as her mother. "Chances are a sheriff in a town like Grass Valley has a beer belly, chews tobacco and has only a passing interest in the offspring of a woman he never knew. I'll have an easy decision to make—he obviously won't be a fit father for the twins—and my conscience will be clear."

Failing that, her last, best hope would be that Eric Oakes wasn't married—at least the detective hadn't uncovered any evidence of a woman in the picture. Amy had been adamant that she didn't want her babies raised by a single father. She didn't trust any man that much.

Laura hugged that thought tightly to her as she kissed her mother goodbye and climbed in behind the steering wheel of the SUV. Amanda and Rebecca were already her life, the children of her heart.

Because she couldn't bear children of her own, they were her one best chance to be the mother she longed to be. They could ease the ache that had been with her since that terrible accident when she'd been sixteen years old—an accident that had been her fault. Oh, she hadn't been driving the pickup truck filled with a half dozen cheering high school friends when a speeding car crashed into them.

But climbing into the back of that truck after their team had beaten the town rivals *had* been her idea. She'd carry that guilt with her forever.

Her hand trembled as she twisted the key in the ignition. Anxiety about what would happen in Grass Valley dried her mouth like a summer drought turns a prairie to dust.

The early-morning sky was a pale blue, the air crystalline clear. The temperature would probably reach seventy-five degrees, typical for July.

Normally she loved driving across Montana during her time off from teaching high school history and government. She'd even been known to go hiking on her own or camping with friends. But this trip—and what might follow—she dreaded at a deeply personal level.

She could lose the babies she had come to love with the intensity that only a mother could possess.

AS SHE'D EXPECTED, six hours later and three stops for diaper changes and bottles, she discovered Grass Valley was little more than a wide spot in a very narrow road.

Laura slowed as she entered the town. Eric Oakes had told her to meet him at his house, so she cruised past the few buildings that lined the main street, noting a couple of women visiting in front of the general store. An older man coming out of the saloon waved at Laura—probably mistaking her vehicle for someone else's. She caught sight of the sheriff's office, a short, stout building that wouldn't even intimidate a jaywalker.

Then she saw the quixotic roadside mailbox, a prisoner in a bronze striped uniform escaping through the roof of the jail. Eric had said she'd have no trouble finding his place.

Drawing a deep breath, she turned into the long driveway leading to a two-story house. Modest by most standards, the best feature was a porch that stretched the full width of the house and was positioned to catch the morning sun. Two wicker chairs promised comfort while watching the sun rise.

A big cottonwood tree shaded portions of the front yard, and beyond the house stood a small barn and corral. A pair of sorrel horses raised their heads to check on her arrival.

Laura didn't want to think about how much Amanda and Rebecca might someday want their own horses or have a swing hanging from a sturdy tree branch. Her townhouse didn't have room for a corral, and the trees were mostly poplars, impossible to climb much less swing from.

When she pulled to a stop, a man came out of the house, the screen door bumping closed behind him as he walked down the steps toward her with an easy stride. Tall and lean in his khaki uniform, he wore a badge pinned to his broad chest and a pager on his belt that was no larger than a trim size thirty-two.

She'd really been counting on a beer belly.

Checking first to see that the twins were still sleeping, she got out of the car.

"Afternoon," he said in the same clear baritone she'd heard on the phone, a tone that held a note of caution.

She nodded. "Sheriff Oakes." His hair—the color of a sand dune after a rainstorm—was cut short, probably to tame the natural waves rather than from any desire to appear military. Crinkles fanned out at the corners of his eyes, as though he'd spent a lot of time squinting into the Montana sky—or laughing. His face was tanned, his jaw square, his lips set in a firm, skeptical line.

"Most folks just call me Eric. We're pretty informal around here." He glanced toward the truck. "You've got the twins with you, Ms…uh…I didn't get your whole name."

"Laura Cavendish. They're in their car seats."

"I wasn't a hundred percent sure you'd show up."

"I said I would."

"Well, let's take a look at 'em." He gestured toward the back seat.

She bristled. "This isn't like picking out a good horse, you know."

His pale-blue eyes narrowed and darkened with suspicion. "I didn't think it was, Ms. Cavendish. But they are my nieces, aren't they?"

"Apparently." More than anything in the world, Laura wished they weren't—wished the detective had made a mistake and traced the wrong man. But he'd assured her that wasn't the case.

"How did you find me, anyway? Johnson is a pretty ordinary name."

"I had your date and place of birth from your sister, which I gave to the detective I hired. Since I knew you and she hadn't been raised together, we guessed you had landed in the foster care system somewhere." The tricky part had been getting ahold of the adoption records. Laura hadn't asked the detective how he'd managed that.

He cocked his brow, then edged closer to her vehicle, peering through the tinted side window. "So you're pretty sure I'm the right guy."

"Yes." She swallowed hard. If she simply got back in the truck and returned to Helena, no one would question that she'd done as Amy had requested and decided their uncle wasn't suitable. The twins would be hers. "But if you're not interested in raising them—"

He grasped the handle and opened the door. Laura held her breath as he leaned inside.

"Oh, my God." He spoke as though his words were a whispered prayer and filled with awe. "They're so little."

Through the crack, Laura saw him tenderly slip his finger into Rebecca's hand. The baby closed her tiny fingers into a fist around him and opened her eyes, looking up at Eric with her bright blue eyes. A bubble escaped her lips.

"Hey, Tinkerbell," he said softly. "This lady says I'm your uncle Eric. Whadaya think, huh?"

The magical exchange between the big, rugged sheriff and his tiny niece was so powerful, Laura's throat closed down tight, and she almost couldn't speak. "That one is Rebecca. The other one is Amanda."

"How do you tell 'em apart?"

"Rebecca's left eyebrow arches a little more than Amanda's does and her ears stick out a tiny bit more. She's also more wakeful than her sister." Somehow, from almost the first moment following their birth she'd been able to tell the twins apart without checking their ID bracelets. The hospital nurses had been amazed. "Other than that, they're identical."

"I'll say."

A light breeze ruffled Laura's hair, shifting it along the back of her neck, and she felt a chill run down her arms. "I think we ought to take the girls inside. They're still a little fragile."

He backed away from the truck. "Oh, yeah, sure. Come on in."

"You get Rebecca, and I'll go around to the other side to get Amanda."

"You want me to—" He blanched as white as if she'd asked him to pick up a deadly snake. "I've never held a baby that tiny before. I'm not sure I know how."

He'd better learn how in a hurry if he expected Laura to even consider leaving the twins in his care for as little as two minutes—forget the rest of their lives.

"Here, let me." She edged past him, acutely aware of what a big man he was. His aura expanded around her, stealing inside her personal space, leaving her feeling slightly breathless. Unsnapping the car seat harness, she lifted Rebecca and gave her a quick kiss. "Come on, Becky. Meet your uncle Eric." She held out the baby to him.

He hesitated.

"She won't break as long as you don't drop her."

"I won't," he promised.

She laid the baby in his arms. "Keep her head propped up. Don't let it fall back."

He looked as awkward as a boy at his first dance, standing as stiff as a robot, not knowing quite what to do with his hands, his expression frozen with fear. Even so, Laura saw he was gentle. His big hand cradled the back of Rebecca's head, his arm held her firmly against his chest.

Not that that meant he'd be a good daddy for the long haul.

"Now, hold her carefully," she warned him again. She hurried to the other side of the SUV, quickly extricating Amanda from her car seat. The infant stretched and yawned, then let out a tiny cry of complaint. "Sorry I had to wake you, Mandy. You're fine, really you are." She grabbed the oversize diaper bag and rejoined Eric, who hadn't budged. "We were going inside?"

"Right." He eyed Laura, then looked down at Rebecca. "I was wrong before. She's not Tinkerbell, she's *Stinker*bell. And I think she's leaking."

"Oh, dear." She stifled a smile at his horrified look. "Well, let's get her inside, and I'll change her diaper. That probably means Mandy is about to let loose, too."

Eric didn't look at all pleased with the prospect. His easy walk that she'd noted earlier turned to a tiptoe race up the porch steps. Despite that, he took the time to hold the door open for her.

An officer of the law and a gentleman—shades of the old west.

For a bachelor's place, the living room looked neat, and the heavy leather couch and recliner gave the room a masculine flavor. In lieu of any feminine touches, there was an overflowing bookcase stuffed with mystery, adventure and science fiction titles, a big-screen TV and a stereo sound system that would rival an outdoor amphitheater. It looked like a case of a boy with plenty of expensive toys.

Noting the row of huge silver rodeo trophies on the mantel above the natural rock fireplace, Laura suspected Eric's music of choice would be country-western. She wondered how he was at two-stepping. Not that she was an expert. Just the opposite. But the dance had always looked like fun.

Holding Amanda in one arm, she pulled a receiving blanket from the diaper bag with her free hand and spread it on the center cushion of the man-size couch. She put Amanda down and reached for Rebecca.

Eric passed her the baby, thinking how odd the

situation felt. A woman in his house and two tiny babies so small he could probably cradle one in each hand like a football if he wasn't so darn scared he'd drop one.

No question, he was going to need a crash course in infant care if they had any chance of surviving under his roof after he was on his own with them.

A father ought to know *something* about taking care of his kids.

If indeed he was a relation at all. He had the feeling he should be waiting for another shoe to drop, one that resembled a complicated con job intended to raid his bank account.

How could anyone know how much he'd always wanted a family of his own?

He watched Laura's swift, confident movements as she changed the babies' diapers. Her head was bent over them, allowing her hair to slide forward, hiding her face behind a ginger-blond screen. Her hairdo was practical, only long enough to reach the angle of her jaw, one of those styles that brushed into place with a few strokes or little more than a shake of her head. But it seemed to shine in the reflected light of the room as though someone had turned a golden spotlight on her.

Her clothes were practical, too. A businesslike navy jacket over a light yellow blouse and navy slacks. Sensible shoes. A long way from a femme fatale or what he'd imagine a scam artist would wear.

She dressed as primly as every social worker he'd ever known as a kid, but something was different about her. When she held one of the twins, murmuring sweet, loving sounds, her smile glowed from the inside out. She had some kind of a special connection to these babies. Eric wasn't sure what.

Granted, he wasn't a big-city cop. But he'd had a fair amount of police training and pretty good instincts. Despite her very attractive packaging, this woman was hiding something.

"Except for knowing my birth name, what other proof do you have that these babies are any relation to me at all?"

Chapter Two

Laura's head snapped up, her eyebrows arched in surprise at his question. "Trust me, Sheriff Oakes, there is no reason in the world why I would lie to you about that."

"But that doesn't mean what you're saying is true. How well did you know the woman who said she was my sister?"

"*Half* sister. You and she had the same mother. I've known Amy since she was ten years old."

"That long?" The more a witness talked, the more likely they were to get their story confused, if they were lying. Eric wanted this woman talking. He wanted the truth.

Rebecca started to fuss, and Laura picked her up, holding her against her shoulder, patting her back. "My mother took Amy in as a foster child when I was about twenty and going to college. I was still living at home, so I was around a lot."

Something dark and painful rose in Eric's chest. "Where was her mother?" *His* mother, if what she was saying was true.

"Amy was being both abused and neglected. Child Welfare removed her from her home and placed her with my mother for her own safety. It was the best thing that could have ever happened to Amy."

God, remembering what had happened to him as a kid, Eric could believe that. "Where is her mother now?"

Laura softened her voice slightly. "She died about five years ago. I'm sorry."

A muscle flexed in his jaw. "I see. You realize I can check your story, don't you?"

She made an impatient sound and plucked a baby bottle from the diaper bag. "Be my guest. The detective's business card is in the truck. And my mother would be happy to give you the name of Amy's former case worker."

Either she was telling the truth, as she knew it, or she was a damn good actress. But the whole story could still be a scam.

Eric sat down on the arm of the couch and watched while Laura slipped the bottle into Rebecca's hungry mouth. She did it with such ease, he guessed she'd done it a thousand times before. Probably. He also noted she wasn't wearing a ring, which likely meant she wasn't currently married.

"What about the twins' father? You know where he is?"

"She never gave me his name. I'm not sure if I knew who he was that I'd go looking for him. She'd gone off with him about a year ago. From what she did tell me, he was abusing her. After she got pregnant, she ran away.''

''Smart woman. But if he knew about her pregnancy, he could still show up and claim his parental rights.'' Eric couldn't think of anything worse than losing his own children. But he couldn't imagine abusing a woman, either.

''I think it's unlikely he'll show up, whoever he is.''

''If Amy knew I existed, I wished she'd tried to find me sooner. I might have been able to help.'' With a restraining order...or something a little more personal and persuasive.

''She didn't know about you, not until shortly before her...death.'' Her voice caught on the word and her chin trembled slightly as though experiencing a painful memory. ''She was going through some old papers of her mother's. That's how she...we learned about you.''

Amanda began twisting and turning on the couch like an eel. Almost immediately she registered her displeasure about something. Eric didn't have a clue what.

''There's another bottle in the bag,'' Laura said. ''Mandy's has a blue top. Can you feed her?''

Panic spiked him in the chest. ''Uh, sure, I guess.''

He found the bottle, gave it a little shake as he had seen Laura do, then stuck it in Amanda's mouth. She started sucking eagerly.

''It would be better if you picked Mandy up and held her while you were feeding her. Cuddling is important to an infant's emotional and intellectual development.''

"Right.'' His brow tightened into a frown. It looked so easy when Laura held and fed Rebecca. In contrast, he didn't know quite where or what to grab on to, and it irritated him that Laura sounded like a baby-care expert.

"You do this for a living?'' he asked. "Taking care of babies.''

"Bigger babies.'' She smiled slightly. "They can cry louder. I'm a high school history and government teacher.''

"Oh.'' Adjusting his position, Eric picked up the baby, bottle and all, cradling her in his arm. She looked up at him with big blue eyes, trusting him as though he could walk on water.

God, did he dare believe these two babies were really related to him? That they were family? That he had a legitimate claim to be their father and raise them?

"What makes you so sure these records you're talking about weren't forged or something.''

"Have you always been this much of a skeptic? Or is it that babies make you that nervous?''

"Come on, you waltz into my life with some crazy story about a sister I never knew I had? Wouldn't you have some doubts, too?'' Less than a year ago a woman had shown up at his brother Walker's house with a baby in tow and claiming to be his new housekeeper. A totally phony story, which had worked out well in the end, he admitted. "A desperate woman looking to find a decent home for her baby can come up with a very convincing lie.''

She leveled him a look that would make most men back off in a hurry. ''I personally guarantee if you don't want to raise Rebecca and Amanda for any reason at all, they will always have a good home—with me.''

The intensity of her words brought him up short. This woman was not fooling around. ''You want to adopt the twins?''

''With all my heart.'' A fine sheen of tears appeared in her eyes, but she didn't let them spill over.

''Then why did you bother to track me down? I never would have known otherwise.''

''Because I promised Amy I would.''

That simple truth, stated with such conviction, had more power than anything else she could have said. She wanted to be the twins' mother. She loved them. Eric was standing in her way. And still she had kept her word to a dead woman—her foster sister.

Removing the bottle from Rebecca's mouth, she lifted the baby to her shoulder again, rubbing her cheek against the infant's blond, fuzzy little head and patting her back.

Assuming the twins were related to Eric, did he have any right to take them away from a woman who so obviously loved them even if it had been their mother's wish that he raise the pair? What the hell had made her—or him—think he was qualified for the job?

Rebecca gave a very unladylike burp, and milk drooled down her chin.

"I brought along the box of records and snapshots Amy discovered. It's in the back of my truck." She laid the baby back down on the couch and wiped the dribble from her lips with the edge of the blanket. "If you'll watch the twins, I'll go get it. Some of the pictures are of you and your mother."

That news drove the air from his lungs. He had nothing of his mother except memories. Some good, some bad. All of which he had tried to repress because the very last memory was of her abandoning him.

LAURA MANAGED to get outside before her chin began to wobble again. She didn't want Eric to see how strongly his interrogation had upset her. It had taken all of her courage to come here to fulfill Amy's wishes. She didn't appreciate being treated like a common criminal. Given a choice, she'd be happy if he decided he wasn't related to the twins, didn't want them around.

But her damn conscience demanded she give him all the information she had before he made up his mind about what he wanted to do.

Sometimes being honest really stank!

Grabbing her slender briefcase from the front seat, she went around to the back of the truck and lifted the hatchback. Her suitcase, baby paraphernalia and a crib filled the back of the SUV. Tucked to one side was a shoe box from a discount store that had long since gone out of business. She took that and a small quilt, carrying them inside.

She found him gazing at the babies but couldn't quite read his expression. It was softer than when he looked at her, more relaxed with at least a trace of awe.

Please don't take my babies away from me.

He looked up at her.

"This is the box with the snapshots and Amy's birth certificate. You'll note the similarity of your mother's name and hers."

Eric held the box in his lap unopened for longer than necessary while Laura busied herself by spreading the quilt on the floor and laying the twins down one at a time. He wasn't sure he wanted to know what was in the box. For the most part, he'd put his childhood behind him. He'd grown up. Whatever faults his mother had had, he didn't dwell on them now.

He didn't want to reopen wounds he'd spent most of his life trying to heal.

One of the babies made a singsong sound, and he realized he had to see whatever Pandora had in mind for him.

The snapshots didn't appear to be in any particular order. A young blond girl in a ponytail standing in front of a pickup truck. The twins' mother, his half sister? A younger version of her on a tricycle. He felt no recognition, no connection.

He picked up the birth certificate and examined it. Amy Maria Thorne, mother listed as Millicent Karen Thorne.

Eric swallowed the tightness in his throat. His mother must have finally found some guy to marry her. She'd been listed Millicent Karen Johnson on his birth certificate. Unmarried.

And then she'd abused and neglected her daughter—just as she had neglected and allowed a ham-fisted man to abuse him.

He caught his breath at the next snapshot, he and his mother standing in front of a roller-coaster ride. He'd been maybe seven or eight at the time.

"I remember this." His voice sounded rusty, his throat was dry. "We'd gone to a county fair. It was the first time I'd ever ridden a roller coaster and some guy with a camera..."

His throat shut down entirely. He couldn't speak, and it felt like someone had tightened a band around his chest, screwing it down hard.

He stood. He had to get away from Laura. Couldn't let her see how upset he was.

With a vague wave of his hand, he fled the room.

Why had his mother abandoned him? What had he done that was so wrong?

Sitting back on her haunches, Laura watched him leave. His obvious pain had brought an ache to her own chest. From what she'd just seen and what Amy had told her, Eric's wounds were fully as deep as his sister's had been.

Smiling down at the twins, who were now chewing on each other's fingers, she silently vowed she wouldn't leave them with Eric until she made sure whatever damage his mother had done to him emotionally hadn't left him so severely scarred that he was incapable of giving the twins the love they deserved.

If she decided to leave them here at all.

When he returned, his strong, masculine features were tightly under control, and he held himself erect.

"You've convinced me," he said. "Amanda and Rebecca are my nieces. We're blood kin, and I'll give them the best home I know how."

Fear and adrenaline drove Laura to her feet. "It's not that easy. I'm not going to simply hand the girls over to you."

"Why not? That's why you tracked me down, isn't it? It's what my sister wanted, right?"

"Not exactly. First, I have to—"

The doorbell chimed, but before either of them had a chance to react, the door opened.

"Hey, Eric, are you home?" a female voice asked.

Laura's heart sank. If Eric had a woman in his life who could be a good mother to the twins—

A young woman with reddish hair swept into the room followed by an equally attractive blonde.

"Oh, look at those sweet little babies," the first one crooned, kneeling beside the quilt on the floor. "Look at their tiny pug noses. They're adorable."

Laura bristled, her protective instincts rising.

Frowning, Eric muttered, "What are you two doing here? And since when do you use the front door?"

"Since we knew you had company and we came to see the babies, of course," the blonde responded. "And to meet the woman you've been seeing on the sly.'' With a welcoming smile, she extended her hand to Laura. ''Hi, I'm Lizzie Oakes, Eric's sister-in-law. And that's Kristi fawning all over your babies, Eric's other sister-in-law. We're both upset he's been keeping you a secret from the family.''

Laura gaped at the woman before finally taking Lizzie's hand. ''I think there's been some misunderstanding. Eric and I haven't been—''

''You don't have to pretend with us,'' Kristi said, playing peek-a-boo with Amanda. ''We're certainly not ones to cast stones.''

''Neither of us,'' Lizzie agreed. ''We just want to make sure Eric is prepared to do the right thing. A woman shouldn't have to—''

''Ladies!'' Eric barked, causing both babies to twist their heads around searching for the source of that unpleasant sound. ''This is Laura Cavendish, who I just met today. And those two babies, who you think are so cute, are my nieces, which is no doubt why you think they're cute. Family resemblance.''

Jaws agape, both young women stared at Eric.

''What sister?'' they said in unison.

''Half sister,'' he admitted. ''Laura, who knew her when she was growing up, brought the twins here so I could meet them. I'm very grateful for that.'' He acknowledged her with a nod. ''And it is my intention, based on my sister's wishes, to adopt the twins and be the best darn father I know how to be.''

''Oh, my…'' Kristi murmured.

''Well, then,'' Lizzie said. ''Congratulations. You'll be a terrific dad.''

"Excuse me, but it's not that simple," Laura told them. She'd been aware via the adoption records the detective had uncovered that Eric had two brothers. She hadn't expected to be assailed right off by two sisters-in-law, however.

"You're right," Kristi agreed, placing a kiss on Rebecca's forehead before she stood. "Among other things, I don't think Eric has a lot of experience with babies. I know he'll be grateful if you could stay here with him for a few days to help him get the hang of things. Unless you have a husband to get home to."

"No, I don't—"

"That's a terrific idea." Lizzie shot a conspiratorial look in Kristi's direction.

Eric stepped forward. "Now wait a minute—"

"You've got that extra bedroom where Laura can stay," Lizzie said. "And the room on the south side will make a wonderful nursery. Sunny and warm in the winter. The babies will love it."

"Trust me, you'll need a lot of extra help at first," Kristi added. "Why, I remember when..."

Laura's head spun as the two women pointed out the importance of having someone on hand who knew how to handle infants. They, the women insisted, didn't have time to help him out. They had their own families. Laura suspected the whole deal was a match-making scheme. On the other hand, she wasn't about to leave the twins in Eric's care just yet. Maybe never. In order to give him a fair chance at proving himself, she needed to give him some time with the babies.

Maybe he'd hate all the inconvenience enough to forget being a father.

Driving through town, she'd noted Grass Valley didn't offer a whole lot of options for temporary housing. She hadn't considered that problem before she left home, and now she had nowhere else to stay except with him and the twins, because she sure as hell wasn't going to leave them.

"I think staying here is a fine idea," she announced.

They all turned toward her. Eric shook his head. Lizzie said, "I think it's perfect, too. Would you like us to help bring in your luggage?"

"No, I'm sure Eric will be more than happy to do that for me." She gave him her stern schoolmarm look that had been known to wither a whole gang of adolescent boys. Managing one man shouldn't be all that difficult.

Lizzie and Kristi appeared pleased they'd accomplished whatever it was they'd set out to do.

"We've got to be running along," Kristi said.

"Just wanted to welcome you to Grass Valley," Lizzie added. "Eric's a great guy, by the way."

Laura smiled weakly. The man had certainly developed a fan club among his sisters-in-law. She wondered what their spouses thought of that. And knew their views wouldn't sway her about leaving the twins with Eric if she wasn't one hundred percent convinced it was the right thing to do.

Given how much she loved the babies, it was hard

to imagine she'd ever be willing to do that, despite Amy's wishes.

She swallowed hard, telling herself she didn't know enough yet about Eric to seriously consider handing over the twins' custody. His worthiness to be their father could take days to determine. Maybe even weeks.

She nearly groaned aloud. Surely it wouldn't take that long to discover some fatal crack in his paragon-of-virtue image.

He managed to escort his sisters-in-law out the door, then returned to the living room.

"I'm sorry about the misunderstanding. Those two are really great people but they do sometimes jump to conclusions."

"It's all right." She knelt and draped a light blanket over the two sleeping babies. "The fact is, you've jumped to a conclusion, too."

"What's that?"

Pulling some papers from her briefcase, she handed a copy of Amy's notarized instructions to Eric.

"Amy was abused most of her life, not just by the man who fathered the twins. The one thing she asked me to do before I relinquished the babies to you is to make sure you had a wife who could love them like a mother should."

He stared at her in disbelief, then quickly read through the papers.

"This makes you the final arbiter of whether or not I get custody."

"That's true." The attorney she and Amy had hired

had carefully crafted Amy's last wishes so that the custody decision about the twins would be Laura's and hers alone.

"And she wanted me to have a wife."

"It was her very strong preference. She had good reasons to—"

"That's crazy!"

"Those were her wishes." She gestured toward the legal papers in his hand. "This is what she wanted. I intend to fulfill her request as best I can."

"Then I guess that makes it you and me against each other."

"If that's how you see it. I see it as doing what's best for the twins."

Chapter Three

"I'm going to need some sort of a changing table."

Sunshine streamed through the window of the designated nursery, but the room itself looked bare, the only furniture the crib Eric had hauled upstairs. There ought to be a border of teddy bear ballerinas dancing along the top of the walls to match the bumper pads and crib sheets Laura had chosen for the twins. An overflowing toy box would fit under the window, a pair of desks in the corner for when they got older, a two-sided easel for painting.

"Seems to me we're short one crib, too," Eric commented, checking that the crib was solidly held together. "They should each have their own."

"For now, they're all right in one. In fact, I think they like it better that way. They seem to want to cuddle as if they were in the womb. When I take them back home—"

"The way I see it, they *are* home. Right here."

"Yes, well..." For a man who'd only lately learned about the twins, he had certainly developed a possessive streak. Or maybe he was challenging her because he was innately competitive. Given the number of rodeo trophies on the mantel downstairs, he wasn't one to give up easily. "That's yet to be determined, isn't it?"

"A court might decide my claim has more merit than yours, given my relationship with the twins."

"You're welcome to consult with an attorney." She and Amy had already done that. In general, the mother's wishes would prevail.

"I think I'll do that tomorrow. Assuming you don't mind staying with the babies while I drive into Great Falls and back."

"If you're planning to raise the twins, you'd better get used to having to take them with you wherever you go."

His brows slammed down into a straight line, narrowing his eyes. "Now you're telling me I'll be disqualified as a father if I use a baby-sitter?"

Laura was sure Eric knew how to smile, but she had yet to see him accomplish the maneuver. But then, her comment had been unreasonable. "Point taken. I'll stay with the twins while you check with your attorney."

Before her accident, Laura had had adolescent dreams of someday finding a man as protective of her as Eric appeared to be of the twins. But as she'd grown older and finally fallen in love, she'd learned the truth. She was damaged goods, a woman no man would want to marry. She couldn't bear his children.

She swallowed back the bitter memory. A man as

macho as Sheriff Oakes would demand nothing less than perfection.

"Come to think of it," Eric said, "who watches the twins when you're at work?"

She cut him a sharp look. Fair was fair, she supposed, and he had a right to know what arrangements she'd made for the twins. "My mother will baby-sit the twins during the school year. She lives only a mile from me and adores Mandy and Becky. She loved Amy like her own, and she's always wanted grandchildren but knew, since my accident—"

"Does that mean in order to get custody I have to come up with a loving grandmother, too, as well as a wife?"

"Well, no, I'd never require that of you." Although Laura's mother would be heartbroken to lose the only grandchildren she was likely to have.

He nodded, but his expression didn't soften much. "Now, you were saying you needed something?"

She forced her thoughts back to practicalities. "A changing table. If you've got a card table or something like that I can use, it will do temporarily."

"I haven't done much decorating of the place, it didn't seem important." Until now, he realized. What did a bachelor need with eight rooms filled with furniture? He only used three or four of the rooms himself. But if this was going to be the twins' home, they needed the right equipment. "Come on, we're going shopping."

"For what?"

"I saw some oak chests of drawers at the general

store. Handmade by an old guy east of town. There ought to be one that's the right size. You can help me pick it out. We can put their clothes and stuff inside.'' He headed for the hallway. He could get another crib, too. At least order one from the catalogs Hetty Moore kept around. And he remembered Susie-Q, Lizzie's little girl, had a jumping swing thing. He'd need two of—

''Eric, the babies are about to wake up. They'll be hungry and need their bottles.''

''Oh. Well, okay.'' So he needed to learn their schedules. No big deal. ''We'll feed them and then we'll go.''

''What time does the store close?''

He checked his watch. ''Six o'clock. It's four now.''

''That should give us barely enough time—if the store doesn't have a big selection and you don't linger over your decision.''

His jaw went slack. It took *that* long to get the twins ready to roll? Lord, when he got up in the morning, he shaved, showered, ate breakfast and was on the road in under thirty minutes. How much longer could it take to get two itty-bitty babies organized for a trip of less than a half mile?

IT WAS LIKE PREPARING for an African safari.

There was a diaper bag, extra bottles, a plastic baggie of pacifiers in case the twins began to fuss. Then Laura had insisted that the infant car seats, which only an hour ago he'd taken into the house, had to be transferred to his vehicle. She was right, of course, that the babies' safety was all-important but the seat belts had tangled. Sorting out the mess had taken Eric a full twenty minutes. She'd suggested, with mock sweetness, that they could take her SUV, which had the seat belts already adjusted to the proper length.

Not a chance! They were *his* kids now.

Still, he had to give her credit. While he had battled frustration, she had remained calm. Cuddling the twins and cooing at them. Checking on his workmanship to be sure the babies would be as safe as possible.

A child could do worse than have her as a mother.

Which didn't mean Eric was going to concede the twins' custody to her, not by a long shot. Blood counted.

By the time they all piled into the police cruiser, a black-and-white SUV with a light bar on top—which he'd been forced to drive because his personal vehicle was a pickup truck that didn't have a place for the twins—Eric was exhausted. He suspected Laura was, too. But she was so tight-lipped, he was afraid to comment.

Hell, they would have been better off to carry the babies down the street to the general store. But then, how would they have gotten a chest of drawers back home if he hadn't driven the SUV?

Not that there was much time left before the store closed to do their shopping by the time they got there.

LAURA ADJUSTED AMANDA in a cuddly sling across her chest. She had yet to find a sling to handle both babies at once, so Eric carried Rebecca into the general store.

A cheery chime greeted their arrival as he pushed open the door and held it for Laura.

An amazing array of products, from wilted produce to bathroom faucets, cluttered the narrow aisles. Aging Christmas items were still on display on the higher shelves, two-foot-tall aluminum trees, dusty Styrofoam snowmen in jaunty hats and a plastic crèche missing its wise men.

Idly Laura wondered how many years the decorations had been waiting for a frantic last-minute shopper to succumb to desperation.

From the back of the store, a woman appeared. She wore a blue butcher's apron over a print dress and had one of those faces that was best described as having character. Laura guessed a line had been etched for each of the seventy-something years she had lived in Montana.

"Afternoon, Eric. Bet you've run out of frozen dinners again and don't want to eat at—" Her eye caught the baby in his arms, and she halted abruptly. "My sakes, look at what you've got. Isn't she the cutest little thing."

Laura winced as the woman chucked Rebecca under the chin. She'd been told by the doctor that the twins' immune system might not be as strong as those of a higher birth-weight baby, and she hated to take the twins around strangers.

"Excuse me," Laura said. "The babies are—"

"Hetty, I'd like you to meet Laura Cavendish. Hetty Moore and her husband, Joe, own the store."

Laura smiled politely, but before she could prevent it, Hetty had zeroed in on Mandy's rosy cheek, giving the baby a grandmotherly pinch.

"Twins…" she crooned. "You've been keeping secrets from us, Eric. Shame on you. These little bundles are too precious to hide. And their mamma, too. Such a pretty girl."

"I didn't know about them till yesterday, Hetty."

"He's their uncle," Laura tried to explain.

Hetty's eyes widened and she gasped. "You mean Walker has been—surely not Rory. Why, they're only just married, the both of them. I can't think what gets into a man's head these days. My Joe and me—"

"Hetty! It's not what you think. This has nothing to do with my brothers."

She huffed. "I should hope not."

Eric rolled his eyes, and Laura stifled a smile. The good folks of Grass Valley had a tendency to jump to conclusions. Explaining the situation would likely take hours, and there wasn't that much time before the store closed.

"Eric was hoping to buy a small chest of drawers to put the twins' things in," Laura said.

"With two new babies to manage, you'll be needing a lot more than one chest of drawers." On a mission now, Hetty bustled down the aisle toward the back of the store.

"They may not be staying that long," Laura called, hurrying after her.

"Now, honey, you don't have to play coy with me, giving me some wild story about young Eric being the twins' uncle. If he's their daddy, you have to give him a chance to make up for whatever he did that upset you. I'm sure you two can work out your differences."

"We might as well give it up for now," Eric muttered only loud enough for Laura to hear. "Once Hetty gets something in her head, it sticks there like Super Glue, even if it's wrong."

"I don't want people to think you and I—"

"They won't. Not for long."

Just what did that mean? Was he going to take out an ad in the local paper, assuming there was one, to explain the situation? Or was it simply too obvious the handsome town sheriff wouldn't be caught dead with someone like her? Not that she was a dog. But she certainly wasn't model thin. Nor had she ever been considered sexy. Men had never fallen all over themselves to ask her out. And the few who had soon lost interest, either because she knew more about history and government than they did, or because she couldn't give birth to the offspring their egos demanded a woman produce.

"Now here's a nice one." Hetty scooped a display of American flags and red, white and blue bunting off the top of a five-foot high honey-oak chest of drawers. "Conrad Gelb's a true craftsman. I'm sure he'd make up another one just like this if—"

"It's too tall," Laura said. "I'm going to use it for a changing table while I'm here."

"He could make you one of those, too, if you want."

"We aren't a hundred percent sure the babies will be staying—"

"I'm sure." Juggling Rebecca in one arm, Eric lifted the edge of a dust cover from a similar oak piece that was about waist high and had three drawers. "How about this one?"

Laura nodded. "That would work fine."

"Won't hold but a teaspoon's worth of baby clothes," Hetty warned.

"We'll take it." Eric glanced around the store. "How 'bout those swing things babies like?"

To Laura's dismay, and frequently over her objections, Eric went on a shopping spree that would have made most women envious. It made Laura uneasy. She didn't like the thought of anyone wasting money. And she didn't like the idea that Eric was so determined to provide everything possible the twins could want or need. In the long run, that attitude wouldn't be healthy for the twins.

Short term, it would make it all the harder to put the babies back in her car and take them away from Eric.

Finally running out of steam, Eric handed Rebecca off to Hetty, who cuddled, cooed and happily pinched the baby's cheeks.

Joe Moore, Hetty's big, burly husband, who looked nothing like a storekeeper, was called from the back room to help carry the purchases out to the car.

Laura had the distinct feeling she and the babies

had been dropped into the middle of a fast-moving stream at flood stage and were being carried along by the current. A helpless feeling and inherently dangerous.

ERIC PLACED the oversize teddy bear near the crib, fluffed its polka-dot bow and stepped back to admire his work. He'd brought everything up from the car. The low chest of drawers was in place across from the windows. The wind-up, jumping-rocking swing was at the closet end of the room right next to an oak rocking chair. Hetty had told him all moms needed a rocking chair.

A dad would, too, he reasoned, smiling. Yep, he'd done all right for his first day as a father.

The cry of a baby preceded Laura's arrival in the nursery, one of the twins in her arms. He couldn't tell them apart yet but he would soon enough.

She handed him the baby. ''Mandy needs a change.''

''You want me to do it?''

''It comes with the territory, Sheriff. Spending money does not a father make.''

''I know that,'' he mumbled. ''It's just that I haven't ever—''

''Changed a diaper. I suspected as much. It's time for your first lesson.''

''Maybe I ought to watch first.''

''Hands-on is the best way to learn, and Becky dozed off after her bottle, so this is a good time. Unless you'd like to wait until they're both fussing.''

"You have a vindictive streak, don't you?" He carried Mandy to the dresser and laid her on the thick pad he'd bought for this very purpose. He should have known Laura would make him initiate the darn thing.

Laura's smile was all too smug. "Possibly."

Almost immediately, Mandy began to fuss and kick her little legs.

"Hold still, Twinkle-Toes." He managed to unsnap the legs on the pink-and-white sleeper but had trouble getting the toes unhooked. "Hey, Sweet Cheeks, how 'bout a little cooperation for your old man?"

Mandy's crying increased in volume.

Eric began to sweat. "Feel free to help out anytime you feel like it."

"You're doing fine."

Like hell! A little more struggling and he got one foot out. The second came easier. He gave Laura a grim smile of accomplishment. "Now what?"

"Take the old diaper off, use a wipe and put on some lotion so she doesn't get a rash."

It all sounded so easy the way she rattled off the instructions.

By bending Mandy's legs over the top of her head, he got the old diaper off. He needed a third hand to reach the new diaper, and by the time he got that more or less in place, he realized he hadn't done the wipe and lotion part. So he started again.

By now Mandy was pretty frantic, little sobs lifting her chest.

He opened the diaper, did a swipe, spread the lotion, reconnected the sides to the front with the sticky tabs and lifted Mandy, smooching her on the forehead, quieting her immediately.

He exhaled in relief, giving Laura a triumphant smile. And the diaper slipped down around Mandy's ankles.

Laura's stern, disapproving expression cracked. He'd thought of her eyes as an ordinary shade of pale blue, and they suddenly sparkled with amusement—at his expense—and he decided they held an amazing depth. Her smile was like a sunrise after a stormy night when the dark clouds had finally lifted. Her laughter reminded him of a lyrical songbird, light and airy. The uncanny transformation flustered and bewildered him. Beneath her tough-as-nails, I'm-the-teacher exterior lurked an entirely different woman.

A woman a man might have trouble resisting—if she were interested.

"I'm sorry." She covered her mouth to silence her laughter, and he was sorry she'd hidden her beautiful smile. "It's just that you looked so—"

"Ridiculous. I know."

"No." Her gaze softened. "Endearing. You were trying so hard, and then—"

"Yeah. I sort of made a mess of things." Except now Mandy had her head buried against his neck, sucking on his collar, and seemed as contented as a baby could be. That part felt good.

"Perhaps we should start again and begin with me showing you the basics."

He met her gaze, nodding. "Starting again sounds

like a great idea." He didn't limit his thoughts to simply starting over with basic baby-care lessons.

SHE SHOULD HAVE PAID closer attention to Hetty's comment about Eric eating frozen dinners.

Laura gazed into the refrigerator at the meager contents. A gallon of milk, a six-pack of beer, some eggs, two apples—one of which was already half rotten—and an assortment of condiments.

"I'm not much of a cook," he admitted. "Most of the time I grab a burger and fries over at the saloon. Or stick something in the microwave."

She opened the freezer and found the selection pretty much limited to pot pies and lasagna. "You might want to consider adding fresh vegetables to your diet."

One side of his lips kicked up into a half grin. "Guess I'll have to be a good example to the twins, huh?"

Now that he'd stopped glaring at her all the time, he looked less formidable. Which didn't make him any less dangerous. More so, since he was so set on being a good father.

"I'll treat you to chicken pot pies tonight," he said. "Tomorrow I'll pick up some fresh stuff when I'm in Great Falls. Hetty doesn't have a real good selection."

"I noticed."

While Eric started dinner, Laura surveyed the spacious kitchen. The twins were in their car seats in the middle of a long oak picnic-style table with benches, probably crafted by the same man who had made the chest of drawers upstairs. The cabinets were a darker wood and needed a face-lift as did the tile counters. But there was a big window over the sink that faced west. It was dark now but Laura suspected it would provide a view of some spectacular sunsets.

"How long have you been sheriff?" she asked Eric while she tickled Rebecca's tummy with one finger. Her reward was a wide, gummy smile.

"About five years. Before that I was on the rodeo circuit."

"I noticed the trophies." How could she not when they were on such prominent display?

"I had some Best-All-Around years until I took one too many headers off a bronc named Lucifer. I broke my leg in three places. Now I've got a couple of pins that set off security alarms in airports." Still in his uniform, he stood with his back to the counter, one booted ankle crossed over the other, looking very much at ease. "I had to stay off my feet for six months, so I moved back to the Double O Ranch. About the time I was mobile again the former sheriff announced his retirement. I decided settling down was a good idea."

"But not on the ranch?"

"Walker enjoys punching cows a lot more than I ever did, and he's a good manager. Rory and I still have an interest in the place, though, and help out during roundups, that sort of thing."

"I gather no woman wanted to settle down with you?"

His eyes immediately narrowed, and Laura regretted she'd asked such a personal question. It wasn't that she was prying, exactly. Knowing something of Eric's past, including his recent history, would help her decide if he was suitable to be the twins' father.

"I've never met a woman I wanted to ask." He held her gaze, the microwave humming its monotonous note behind him. "How about you? Have you ever been married?"

She swallowed hard and turned back to the twins. Mandy had spit out her pacifier; Laura plugged it back in. "I came close once. It didn't work out."

"What went wrong?" His voice was a little softer than it had been. Intimate.

Her past was none of his business, except maybe he'd understand better why she was so reluctant to turn over the twins to a stranger. Why she wanted to be their mother.

"He wanted to have a son to carry on the family name." Lifting her head, she looked at him levelly despite the painful knot in her stomach. "I can't have children. I was in an accident and they had to remove my uterus."

His mouth went a little slack. "I'm sorry."

"No more than I am." She forced a shrug she hoped looked casual. "The worst is, they left the rest of my female parts, so I get the joy of PMS without any of the benefits."

The buzzer on the microwave saved him from responding to her revelation. Just as well. Laura didn't want his sympathy.

She wanted a reason, even a small one, to salve her conscience so she could reject him as a suitable father for the twins and raise them herself. After meeting Eric, that had to be the most selfish thing she'd ever wanted in her life.

DINNER didn't go well.

Laura explained to Eric the uncanny knack the twins had for turning fussy the moment anyone sat down to eat a quiet meal. Eric found himself cradling Becky in the crook of his left arm while trying to fork a bite or two of pot pie into his mouth without dribbling the hot gravy on the baby. Not an easy task.

She couldn't have babies of her own. No wonder she was so damn anxious to keep the twins for herself. As much as he might sympathize, that didn't mean he had to hand them over to her. His sister had wanted him to raise her babies. It made sense that they'd live with a blood relative.

As a kid in foster care, Eric had spent hours fantasizing about an uncle or aunt or grandparent who'd show up and give him the home he'd dreamed of having. His *own* family. But nobody came.

He wasn't going to let that happen to Mandy and Becky. It didn't matter how much Laura loved or wanted to raise them. Or that she'd been Amy's *foster* sister.

She wasn't *real* family.

By the time they'd finished eating, the babies were ready for another bottle. That was followed by a change of diapers and clean sleepers. Tomorrow,

Laura warned, she'd give him a lesson in bathing the babies. It was too late now.

"Do you want to do the next feeding on your own?" she asked as she placed Mandy in the crib next to Rebecca. Magically, the pair gravitated toward each other.

"What time does that happen?"

"Usually between one and two. Then they wake again around five."

"How are we supposed to get any sleep?"

She gave him a wry smile that said sleep wasn't a part of the deal.

"I'll handle both feedings," he said generously. "You've been up since early morning." Of course, he hadn't been out to feed his horses yet this evening, and there were still dinner dishes to do. But there weren't many and they could wait until morning. He'd put them in the sink to soak. No big deal.

She arched her brows. "If you're sure."

"I'll have to manage sooner or later. I might as well start now. I'll call you if I run into trouble."

With a shake of her head, Laura told him goodnight and headed toward the guest room. He was the most determined man she'd ever met. She suspected, however, it was a case of a fool rushing in when an experienced person would be more wary. Granted, he'd pretty well gotten the hang of changing diapers and could fix a bottle, but in the middle of the night his new skills might not come all that automatically.

The spare bedroom looked as though it had once

belonged to a teenage girl, the white antique furniture and twin bed with a pink flounce likely left behind by the prior owners. It smelled musty, and she opened the window to let in some fresh air. The scent of sage and lush summer grass wafted in the window.

The faint glow of starlight shadowed the rolling landscape and outlined the nearby barn and corral. Unlike her home in Helena, where there was always the sound of neighbors coming or going and the hum of traffic on the boulevard, here silence enveloped the night. It pressed in on her ear drums, sending a message of loneliness that was more easily ignored when drowned out by the presence of others.

The sound of the back door opening broke the quiet, and she caught sight of Eric striding toward the barn. The horses in the corral whickered a soft greeting, moving in the same direction. No matter how tired he might be, caring for his animals came before his own comfort.

She pressed her lips together. Given a chance, he'd do the same for the twins.

Turning away from the window, she opened her suitcase and pulled out her cotton nightgown. She'd been busy all day and was too weary to unpack now. When she'd left home, she had hoped she wouldn't be staying long in Grass Valley, wouldn't need to settle in.

In the face of Eric's determination to be a father, that goal seemed less attainable now.

The next day or two—or maybe one sleepless night

up with crying infants—would tell the tale of his resolve.

She'd hope for the best—or perhaps it was the worst she was looking for in the twins' sleeping habits.

ERIC WENT TO SLEEP making plans to hang an old tire as a swing from the cottonwood tree out front when the twins were old enough.

He woke to the wailing sound of the smoke alarm.

He was on his feet, pulling on his pants, before he realized it was the twins crying. How could two tiny sets of lungs make that much noise?

Shaking the fuzziness from his head, he stumbled out of the bedroom into the hallway. He met Laura at the door to the nursery.

"I've got 'em," he mumbled, his voice thick with sleep.

"Becky's been crying for five minutes. She woke up Mandy."

"Sorry. I didn't hear 'em." How could Laura tell which one was crying, for Pete's sake? It just sounded like a racket to him.

They both bent over the crib, each one picking up a baby, which quieted the infants only briefly. Eric followed Laura downstairs, where she retrieved two bottles from the refrigerator, where she'd had him place them earlier, and popped them into the microwave. Jiggling the baby in his arms, he stared stupidly at the glow of the oven until it buzzed.

They each took a bottle and sat down next to each

other on the bench at the kitchen table. A moment later the screams were replaced by the sound of eager little sucking noises, not unlike a newborn calf discovering his source of sustenance for the first time.

Eric sighed in relief.

"After a while you get tuned in to their cries and wake up at the first peep. It's better not to let them get too upset."

He grunted noncommittally. That kind of adjustment might take more than a day or two.

Gazing at nothing in particular, his eyes finally focused on Laura's feet. Her *bare* feet. Long, slender toes tipped by polish in a rainbow of bright colors, each toenail a different hue.

He grinned, awake now. "Nice toenail polish."

"Huh? Oh." She folded one foot over the other like a shy little girl. "My neighbors have a nine-year-old daughter who wanted to try out her new fingernail polishing kit."

"And you volunteered?"

"Something like that."

He let his gaze wander higher, surveying the modest nightgown she wore buttoned securely at her throat. He had the oddest urge to slowly undo the gown one button at a time to discover what other surprises were hidden behind her prim exterior.

He'd never had a woman stay overnight in his house. It had never seemed to be the right time. The right woman.

Having Laura here was definitely going to challenge his view of what was "right"…and what was wrong for both him and her.

Chapter Four

Frustration had Eric clenching his teeth by the time he finished his meeting with the attorney the next day. He called his brothers and asked them to meet him at the ranch. Maybe they could help him figure out how to get over or around the custody plan for the twins.

The heart of the Double O had always been the office Oliver Oakes had used. That was the place where he'd designed successful breeding programs, determined how many head of beef cattle had to be culled in the fall so the herd would survive until spring with the available feed…and where his adopted sons were called onto the carpet for their misdeeds.

Walker sat behind the heavy oak desk now, reading Amy Thorne's instructions regarding the future of her children. Rory lounged in the leather chair in the corner, contemplating the problem while Eric paced.

Walker set the papers aside. "That's crazy."

"My thought exactly," Eric said. "Unfortunately, the attorney says it will probably stand up in court. I could appeal, but the twins would be going to their first prom before any higher court heard the case. Meanwhile, Laura would be raising them.'' He didn't have to explain why the twins were important to him. He and his brothers had all dreamed of having their own families. For Walker and Rory that dream was coming true.

Not so for Eric.

Leaning forward and linking his hands between his knees, Rory said, ''I don't suppose it would be a good idea to put a price on Laura's head and let my Indian brothers know about it.''

Walker shot Rory a quelling look. ''Not funny, Bird Brain,'' he said, using the nickname he and Eric had chosen for Rory following his Blackfeet naming ceremony when he'd become Swift Eagle. They had decided it was far too classy sounding for their troublesome brother. ''Among other things, Lizzie tells me Laura is a nice lady. Very attractive.''

''She is,'' Eric agreed.

''I don't get why she's so damned anxious to raise somebody else's kids, though,'' Rory commented.

''She has her reasons.'' Eric didn't feel any need to reveal Laura's personal problems. That was her own private business.

''I've got a gaggle of kids Lizzie and I are raising who weren't born to us,'' Walker pointed out. ''Children have a way of getting under your skin when you're not watching.''

At this point, Walker and his wife of a year were raising six children, four of them teenage boys plus one preschooler and a toddler. Eric expected someday soon they'd get around to having a baby of their own and expand their family again.

He sat on the edge of Walker's desk. "The point is, I want to be a father to Amanda and Rebecca. Raise them. But I don't see how I'm going to do that unless I can magically pull a wife out of a hat somewhere."

His brothers were quiet for a moment, then Rory said, "You aren't bad-looking for a white-eyes. There've got to be a lot of women who'd be willing to marry you."

"Thanks for your vote of confidence," he muttered.

"How much time is Laura Cavendish giving you to come up with a wife?" Walker asked.

Eric shrugged, feeling defeated. "We haven't talked about a deadline."

"Well, that's the answer, then." Rory shoved back from his desk and stood. "While you're learning to be a daddy, Rory and I will help you find a wife."

"We will?" Rory asked.

"Sure. It shouldn't be too hard. Like you say, he's not bad-looking and there are a lot of girls out there wanting to tie the knot. Most of 'em even like babies."

"Now wait a minute," Eric protested. "I don't want to end up with just any woman. I'd like a choice, okay?"

"It all depends on how much you want custody of those babies. If you can drag out your training time and keep Laura around long enough, Rory and I will get you all the candidates you can handle.''

''I don't know...''

Walker tucked his fingertips in his hip pockets. ''I don't see you have much of a choice, bro. You've got to give it a shot.''

HE'D REMEMBERED TO STOP at the grocery store.

Laura watched through the window as he unloaded a couple of sacks from his pickup truck. Knowing what his attorney in Great Falls had no doubt told him, she was surprised he had bothered. But then, she'd already discovered Eric Oakes was a responsible man.

Sighing, she considered how unfortunate it was that Amy and Eric's mother hadn't had the same attribute. Then the siblings might have been raised in an intact family. Which is exactly what Amy had desperately wanted for her babies.

Laura knew she could give them stability, if not a two-parent family. So could Eric, she supposed. But Amy had been leery of all men. She'd never found one she could trust.

Except for her father, neither had Laura. Not when it came down to the nitty-gritty.

Swallowing the familiar sense of grief tinged with guilt for her part in her father's heart attack, she opened the back door and held it for Eric. ''Hope you got lots of salad makings.''

''Lettuce, tomatoes, cucumbers, onions, baby carrots, croutons, the works, plus enough squash for a night or two. I didn't know what kind of dressing you'd like, so I picked out a couple." He set the sacks on the kitchen table. "Got some fruit, too. Mostly apples and oranges. The apricots looked too green."

She was impressed. Not many men could shop like that, particularly without a list to go by. "Sounds good to me."

"There's some chicken and ground beef, a couple of steaks."

"Wonderful."

He began to pull things out of the bag and stuff them in the refrigerator. She'd have to wash the produce later. For now she'd be happy with the prospect of a balanced diet.

"Did you talk to your attorney?" she asked.

"I did." He put two packages of ground meat in the freezer on top of a frozen lasagna. She noted the meat had been packed in a thermal sack to keep it cold for the trip home.

Laura waited for his concession of defeat. Amy's wishes would prevail in a court of law. The family friend and attorney she'd hired, Bill Williams, had assured Laura there would be no way to challenge Amy's assignment of the twins' guardianship to her. Eric put everything away, folded the sacks and crammed them in with a dozen others under the sink before he turned toward her.

"I agree to Amy's terms."

She blinked, not quite understanding his words. "Her terms?"

Taking his usual pose, he leaned back against the

counter and crossed his arms. "Amy wanted me to adopt and raise the twins but only if I had a wife who could be a good mother to them. Right?"

An uncomfortable feeling crept down Laura's spine and she straightened. "That's correct."

"Then I agree to those terms. I'll get married."

She had to swallow a gasp, of surprise or dismay, she wasn't sure which. "You have a woman—"

"I'll find one."

"You think it will be that easy?"

"My brothers are going to help me."

"They're going to help you find a wife?" She gasped. What kind of a crazy scheme had they cooked up? An Internet dating service? A wife-in-name-only until Laura was out of the picture?

"How much time will you allow me to comply with Amy's wishes?"

"Well, I can't—" She faltered. She had come here hoping to find Eric didn't want the babies at all. Or that he was immediately unsuitable. Not for a minute had she expected him to race out and find a wife simply to gain custody of the babies. *Her* babies! "I don't know. I've applied for a curriculum coordinator's job. I expect to hear in a week or two." The job would give her more flexibility than classroom teaching and wouldn't pose the problem of hiring a substitute if she had to stay home with the twins. It would also offer a new set of challenges, creating ways to entice young people to care enough about history so they might not want their country to repeat the mistakes of the past.

"Then I'll find a wife in that amount of time."

"You can't! It would be impossible to—"

"Nothing is impossible if you want it enough."

The way he looked at her, the intensity in his pale-blue eyes, told her he believed just that. Within two weeks he was going to find a wife; one she would find suitable as the mother of the twins. The thought was crazy, entirely irrational.

An irritating voice in her head suggested he was capable of doing anything he set out to do. He was *that* determined.

"I could take the twins back home and let you call me when you found someone."

"*This* is their home, and you believe in fair play. You'll stay."

She licked her lips. Damn him! She did believe in fair play, but she should be able to overcome that dubious personality trait when she loved and wanted the twins so much.

Slowly she nodded. "Until I have to get back to Helena for the new job." Assuming the superintendent picked her. "Then all bets are off."

The grim set of his jaw said that was one bet he intended to win.

ERIC'S CHIN DROPPED to his chest and he jerked himself awake. Three nights of sleep depravation was not a good thing.

He glanced longingly at the hard cot in the jail cell behind him. If he lay down now, he'd conk out until tomorrow morning. He'd never get his month-end paperwork done, and he'd give Laura more ammunition to prove he wasn't a suitable father.

How did single dads manage on their own?

Rubbing his eyes, he stood and walked to the window. The street was pretty quiet. Abe Miller at the garage was pumping gas into Karl Huhn's old station wagon. Down the street, John Jones's pickup was parked in front of the saloon along with a couple of cars he didn't recognize. Out-of-towners, he guessed.

Since the day was pretty well shot, anyway, he decided to go home and start again on the monthly reports tomorrow. If anyone needed him, the office phone rang in the house and he always had his pager turned on.

Locking up, he got into the cruiser to drive the short distance to his house. As a precaution he kept the vehicle secured in his own garage at night, handy if he needed it and not an easy target for kids who had mischief on their minds.

He slipped into the house through the back door, where the scent of cinnamon and apples caught him off guard. A freshly baked pie sat on the counter. Homemade, by the looks of it.

His mouth watering, he went in search of Laura. He found her in the living room.

The twins were asleep on a blanket she'd spread on the floor near the window, a collection of rattles and stuffed animals spread around them. Laura was curled beside the babies, her slender form providing a protective arch as she slept on her side with her head on her outstretched arm.

The length of her delicate neck was exposed in sensual invitation as her hair fell forward. The curve of her hips pulled her jeans snugly across her nicely rounded bottom, a perfect spot for a man to rest his hand and gently flex his fingers. Her brightly painted toenails winked at him with a hint of both humor and passion.

The juxtaposition of a sexy woman in a thoroughly maternal pose plucked at something equally masculine in Eric. A reaction he tried to ignore and failed.

Sitting down on the arm of the couch, he purposefully switched his attention to the babies. They lay on their backs, arms and legs splayed in a relaxed pose, their tiny hands just touching. Two little Cupid's bow mouths worked wordlessly as though they were both dreaming of the perfect bottle.

Hey, kids, I'd like to be your dad. Whadaya think?

The enormity of becoming an instant father weighed down on him. What if he messed up? A thousand things could go wrong when you raised children. Particularly a single man with two little girls.

Maybe Amy had been right to insist he have a wife. Except, his brothers had yet to produce even one candidate. But that didn't mean he'd easily give up on being a dad.

Laura stirred, stretched and blinked her eyes open. She rolled onto her back and started when she saw him.

Eric touched his finger to his lips.

"You're home early." Pushing up to a sitting position, she shook her arm and rubbed at it as though it had gone to sleep.

"I was so tired I wasn't getting any work done at the office."

"The nighttime feedings can really get to you."

"How have you been managing for three months?" For him, it had only been three days. He couldn't imagine being this exhausted for that long.

"Coffee. Black. Gallons of it. And I did take a leave of absence from teaching. Naps are good."

Even so, she was one strong lady. Maybe nature gave women a maternal gene that let them survive for months at a time with little or no sleep. Next time he'd stand in that line, too.

"You baked a pie," he commented. "Smelled good when I came in."

She levered herself up to sit on the edge of the couch. "The twins and I went to visit Hetty this morning. She had some apples on sale. Couldn't pass them up. Besides, I like to bake."

"That's a nice coincidence because I like to eat home-baked pies. Home-baked anything, for that matter."

"I thought you might."

They shared a companionable smile that went a little deeper than friendship and held no trace of the battle they were waging for custody of the twins.

His gaze shifted to the sleeping babies. "What was my sister like?"

She hesitated, her attention following his to the infants. "She was almost painfully shy when she came to us. Afraid of what was happening, afraid she'd be sent back where she came from, I suppose.''

He remained silent, hating that his mother had treated his sister so poorly. Hating that he hadn't been there to help Amy.

''I think Amy warmed up to me sooner than to my mother,'' Laura said. ''She used to love fussing with my makeup. Sometimes I'd do her hair up on top of her head, princess-style. We'd all go to movies together. She liked that.''

''She was lucky she found a good home.'' Just as he'd finally landed with Oliver Oakes.

''I was getting older and my mother needed someone to mother. Amy gave her that opportunity.''

''Was she smart? You know, a good student?''

''She was smarter than her grades reflected, I suspect. Her favorite class in high school was choir. She was a lovely, clear soprano. Not a big voice, but she did get to sing a couple of solos. She was thrilled—and terrified.''

He chuckled. ''That must not be genetic. Growing up, if I sang in the shower, my devoted brothers turned off the hot water to get me out of there.''

She looked at him, surprised. ''You have a very nice speaking voice. I would have thought—''

The shrill sound of the phone ringing shattered the moment. Eric bolted toward the kitchen in the hope he'd get there before the jarring noise woke the babies.

Laura fell to her knees as Rebecca's eyes flew open. So did her mouth. Laura stuck a pacifier in. The twins had only been sleeping for a half hour or so. If they woke up now, they'd be even fussier than usual during dinner. And Becky had an uncanny way of insisting if she was going to be awake and miserable, her sister should be, too.

Laura rubbed the baby's tummy, watching in relief as Becky's eyes fluttered closed again.

In the background, she could hear Eric talking on the phone. When she'd awakened and rolled over, finding Eric staring down at her and the twins, her heart had lodged in her throat. There'd been a softness in his gaze that had both startled her and sent a low, curling heat through her midsection.

She rarely experienced a sensation like that. In recent years, since her breakup with Gary Swanson, she'd avoided any thought of wanting a man. She didn't want to be hurt again. Couldn't bear the possibility of a man telling her she was damaged goods.

But Eric had sneaked up on her when her guard was down. And he did have the nicest baritone voice that could lull a woman into thinking about things she shouldn't.

Living together carried with it a false sense of intimacy, particularly the late-night feedings they shared, the house quiet, Eric bare-chested. Her imagination far too active.

She was trying—no doubt foolishly—to give him a chance to prove he was a fit father for the twins. She couldn't confuse their unusual situation with anything resembling a personal relationship. They were still vying for opposite goals. Her own personal reactions were irrelevant under the current conditions.

He returned to the living room, walking softly. He spoke the same way.

"That was Kristi on the phone. She and Lizzie want to throw us a baby shower on Sunday, after church. The congregation will put together a potluck."

"Are you sure you want to involve that many people? When I take the twins back to Helena—"

"I'm going to find a wife, remember?"

"Are there prospects at church?"

"Maybe," he said grimly. "If nothing else, there are a whole lot of folks in this town who'll help me out with the twins if I need them."

Laura suspected that was true. But it wasn't the same as having two parents.

The phone rang again, and she grimaced as Mandy woke this time. The nap was pretty much over, she guessed.

A minute later she had Mandy in her lap when Eric reappeared.

"We've got some vandals knocking over mail boxes out on Settlers Road. I've got to go check it out."

"When do you think you'll be back?"

He shrugged noncommittally. "I don't know. Save some pie for me."

"I will." She remembered her father being called back to work to handle a crisis or having to work overtime. He'd been a city cop, but the job was the same. You went when you were called.

Which was another reason Eric wouldn't be a good choice as a parent if he didn't have a wife. With his unpredictable schedule, he'd have to hire full-time, live-in help to care for the twins. He couldn't rely solely on his friends and relatives. And child-care workers were notoriously unreliable, often changing jobs or moving away on a whim. The twins would be in the hands of a continually changing series of housekeepers or nannies.

That wasn't what Amy had wanted for her children. No matter how wonderful Eric was with the babies, what a great father he might be, Laura could never approve an arrangement like that.

A HALF HOUR LATER, the twins were in full-throated complaint when the doorbell rang. With Becky taking her turn in the portable swing, Laura carried Mandy to the door. The movement caused Mandy to burp, sending a rivulet of milky spit-up down Laura's shirt. She wiped at it halfheartedly and opened the door.

A perky young blonde in low-riding, skin-tight jeans, a tank top that left her stud-pierced belly button bare and a Stetson with a rhinestone band stood on the porch. "Hi, is Eric around?" she chirped.

"He got called out to investigate some vandalism."

"Oh, well, you know, Rory sent me." She made it sound like a secret password to get into a Depression-era speakeasy. "I'm Crystal, Crystal Lereaux—with an *x*, you know—but everybody calls me Crystal."

"Is there something I can do for you, Crystal?"

The girl looked past her into the house. "Well, like, is he going to be gone long?"

"He wasn't sure."

"Well, like, I mean, maybe I can wait for him?"

By now, Mandy was quiet but Becky was fussing again, so Laura opened the door wider. "Come in, please. As you can see, I'm a little harried at the moment."

"Sure. Whatever."

She walked in, and Laura had to wonder how anyone could walk and wiggle their butt in quite that way. She must not have bones in the same places Laura did.

"You're a friend of Rory's?" Laura managed to switch the twins so Mandy was in the swing, Becky in her arms and quiet again.

"Sort of, you know. I mean, I've seen him around the rodeo sometimes."

Her *you know*s set Laura's teeth on edge. Not that the students in her classes didn't speak the same way. But it wasn't one of their most endearing traits, from Laura's perspective. "Rory wanted you to see Eric?"

"Yeah, like he said Eric was a cool dude, a champion bronc rider and was thinking of getting married."

Laura drew in a sharp breath just as Crystal noticed the trophies on the mantel. Was this woman Rory's idea of a perfect wife for Eric?

"Oh, wow, man, would you look at those chunks of silver! He must'a hit the mother lode!" Crystal wiggled across the room to examine the trophies, stepping right in the middle of the babies' blanket Laura had spread on the floor. She barely avoided trampling a plastic rattle in the shape of a spoon with her hand-carved, high-heeled leather boots.

Laura barely held her tongue at the girl's thoughtless behavior. Eric was thinking of *marrying* this... this little *twit?* Not for all the silver in the world would she hand over the twins to a woman like Crystal.

"So, hey, I mean, does he have any new ones?"

"New ones, like what?" Laura grimaced, her jaw hurting from clenching her teeth so tightly together.

"Like these trophies are ancient history. Isn't he on the circuit anymore?"

"I don't think so." The most recent was only five years old. In Laura's book, that was darn recent. Besides, from what Eric had told her, he'd been seriously injured riding a bronc. Thank goodness he'd had enough sense not to go back on the circuit.

Disappointment melted the girl's chipper expression like a flame melts wax. "Bummer."

With superb timing, Eric chose that moment to appear, coming in the back from the kitchen.

"Hello. I didn't know we had company."

"This young lady is Crystal Lereaux—with an *x.* It seems Rory mentioned to her you were looking for a wife. She was very impressed with your trophies until she realized how *old* they are."

In a quick, sweeping gaze, Eric took in the young woman by the fireplace, probably half his age, and

Laura's disapproving expression as well as her protective hold on one of the twins. What the hell had Rory been thinking?

"Nice to meet you, Crystal. I'm Eric Oakes."

Her eyes widened. "You the law?"

"County sheriff."

"Oh, that's heavy, man. I mean, Rory only said, you know, like you were his little brother."

Eric winced. His brother was going to have a lot of explaining to do next time Eric saw him.

"Crystal, why don't you and I walk over to the saloon? I'll buy you a drink and we can get acquainted."

"You better check her ID first," Laura muttered. She bent down and scooped up the babies' blanket, tossing it onto the back of the couch.

He gestured for Crystal to join him. He was sure she had a false ID, which wasn't going to be necessary. "We won't be long," he said to Laura.

"Don't rush on my account. I'm sure she'll be delighted to hear your *old* rodeo war stories." Her sweet, syrupy voice stung like acid on a reopened wound. It wasn't his fault his brother had picked out a rodeo groupie who was used to riding cowboys with their spurs on. He'd given up that gambit a long time ago.

He ushered Crystal out the door and down the porch steps. She was one hot package, all right, with her tight little rear end, minuscule waist and unrestrained breasts that threatened to fall out of her tank top. But no longer his style, if she had ever been.

Now he was settled, moving all too rapidly toward middle age. He needed a woman with a certain maturity. One who knew how to handle kids, that was for sure.

He definitely didn't want a near juvenile—a rodeo groupie—for a wife.

Coming to a halt beside Crystal's pickup, an extended-cab version with long horns mounted on the hood, he said, "You know, if we have a drink together it may be too late for the long drive you'll have later. Maybe we ought to skip it."

"You're brushing me off?"

"Isn't that what you'd like?"

She looked embarrassed. "I guess. You are a little old for me."

Tell me about it. "I really appreciate you driving all this way, and I'm sure Rory will, too." *Particularly after I plant his head on top of the flagpole in front of the sheriff's office.*

"That's okay. He's a pretty cool dude—for an old guy."

"I'll let him know." He opened the truck door for her, and she climbed into the cab. "Drive carefully."

"I always do." She slipped the key into the ignition and closed the door. "You might want to watch out for the housekeeper you've got, know what I mean? She is like, you know, so not cool."

"I'll be careful." He stepped back from the truck.

Crystal whipped the truck into a U-turn and sped out his drive toward Main Street. Before she was a block away, she'd broken a half-dozen traffic laws.

Eric had no interest in pursuing her in order to give her a citation. Or for any other reason.

He went back into the house. Laura was sitting on the couch with the twins.

"That was a quick drink," she said.

"I plan to have a chat with Rory about robbing the cradle. Crystal agreed we wouldn't be a good match."

A faint smile teased at the corners of her lips. "Did you catch your vandals?"

"Couple of boys from Hill County decided to take a joyride in their dad's pickup after a few too many beers. The sheriff over there locked them up and called their folks."

"Lucky they weren't hurt." She lifted a sleepy baby to her shoulder. "I saved a dinner plate warming for you in the oven."

"And the pie, I hope."

"Help yourself. I think these little ones have finally worn themselves out. At least temporarily. I'm going to put them down for the night."

He hesitated, but only for a moment. "I'll give you a hand." With the same care Laura had shown, he lifted the second twin—Mandy, he thought.

"It's so late, you must be starved."

His stomach rumbled right on cue. "Waiting a few minutes longer won't hurt me, and you've had the kids all day." Besides, he'd kind of missed being with the babies when he was out on the road. They were nice to come home to.

So was Laura, he realized with a start.

For now he didn't want to analyze that thought too

closely. It was enough to recognize the merit of a woman who wasn't half his age, had a vocabulary that included multisyllable words and knew her way around a kitchen.

He didn't need to consider the unguarded moments when his thoughts about her turned to the woman beneath her chaste exterior. The way he wondered how and where she liked to be kissed. And stroked. Or what it would take to arouse the passionate woman he was sure she'd hidden away even from herself.

Chapter Five

She hadn't seen this many vehicles in one place since she left Helena.

The church's parking lot was awash with pickup trucks and SUVs, all of them muddy and many of them sporting fender dings and signs of rust. In comparison, her SUV appeared pristine even though it was three years old and had close to fifty-thousand miles on it.

A bell tower with a lightning rod topped the small whitewashed church, and there were flourishing beds of forget-me-nots, marigolds, snapdragons and baby's breath across the front of the building. There were also lots of people in their Sunday best visiting with friends and neighbors as they waited for the morning service to begin.

Laura managed to get out of the truck and lift Rebecca out of her car seat before Lizzie and Kristi descended on them.

"Hmm, let me get my hands on that precious baby," Kristi said, taking Becky from her.

On the far side of the truck, Lizzie was doing the

same with Mandy, Eric standing out of the way with an amused smile on his face.

Laura picked up the diaper bag from the floor of the back seat. "I brought some double-chocolate brownies for the potluck."

Kristi nuzzled Becky's neck, eliciting an open-mouthed smile in return. "You didn't have to go to all that trouble. You're the guest of honor. Well, the babies are, actually, but you're our guest, too."

"It wasn't any trouble. I like to bake."

"I bet Eric loves that!" Her blue eyes sparkled with delight.

"Well, between the twins' feedings and baths and whatnot, there isn't all that much spare time to make anything fancy. But brownies are easy. I confess I used a boxed mix."

"Bring them along. I'll have someone put them in the rec room. That's where the party will be after the service. For now, we want you to meet the rest of the family." Kristi took off walking with Rebecca propped on her shoulder.

Laura followed, keeping a spare eye on Lizzie, who had a firm hold on Mandy. "I'm not sure how the babies will do in church. They may start crying."

"If they do, one of us will take them outside."

"They should be kept out of drafts." She turned back to Eric. "Can you get the car seats? The babies might be more comfortable if—"

He waved. "I'll get 'em."

Kristi made a beeline for two men in Stetsons, fancy, Western-cut shirts and new jeans who were standing off to the side of the crowd. A toddler circled one of them as though she were on a merry-go-round.

"Honey, didn't I tell you the twins were adorable?"

The taller of the two men, who was clearly of Native American descent, put a possessive arm around Kristi. "If you say so, hon."

Kristi asked Laura, "Which one is this?"

"That's Rebecca," she answered.

Kristi gave the twin a quick kiss. "Laura, I'd like you to meet my husband, Rory. And this is Walker, Lizzie's husband." She nodded toward the second man. "They're Eric's brothers."

Both men politely tipped their hats.

"Yes, I can see the family resemblance," Laura said, straight-faced.

Their smiles froze for a moment, then Walker grinned. "Rory and Eric got all the ugly genes. I got the handsome ones."

"Now, wait a minute," Rory protested. "How 'bout we take a vote on that. Kristi, you go first."

"That's okay," Walker agreed, reaching out for his wife and drawing her closer, along with Becky. "Slick, here, will have the last word, and she'll agree with me." He bent down to pick up the toddler, who had begun tugging on Lizzie's skirt.

"I wouldn't think of interjecting myself into any argument you're having with your brother," Lizzie said. "You're on your own."

Laura, however, wasn't averse to a little screw tightening. "Evidently Rory is the one who thought a rodeo groupie under the age of consent would be a perfect bride for Eric."

"You did?" Kristi looked at her husband accusingly. "Why would you think a thing like that?"

He flushed. "Well, I—"

Eric arrived. "Where do you want the car seats?"

"Put them in the rec room," Kristi said. "And could you get one of the boys to take Laura's brownies in there, too?"

"Not Fridge!" Walker and Lizzie said in unison.

Everyone laughed as Eric walked off, and then Lizzie explained the joke. "We have four teenage sons, whom we've adopted. I'm afraid Fridge has a hollow leg."

"Two of them," Walker added.

Lizzie finished her thought. "It's unlikely he would have enough self-control to avoid finishing off the brownies by himself."

"He's a really sweet boy," Kristi said, defending the youngster. "He came over to fix the autoclave at the clinic the other day."

"And raid the refrigerator?" Walker asked.

It was Kristi's turn to blush, and she shrugged. "I gave him some money for an ice-cream cone at the drugstore. He said he was hungry."

They all had another laugh, but their laughter was so filled with love, Laura couldn't help but think that Fridge had found himself a wonderful home and family.

By now people were moving into the church. A redheaded teenager named Scotty showed up to deliver the brownies to the rec room, and everyone else filed in for the service.

Laura found herself squeezed into a whole pew filled with members of the Oakes family—teenage

boys, a little girl who had to be biologically related
to Scotty, their hair the exact same shade of carrot
red, and Susie, who was the toddler in her father's
arms. A five-year-old, who was obviously Rory's son,
popped up from somewhere to sit next to his father.
Eric eased his way into the pew, taking his place beside Laura. His sisters-in-law continued to claim pos-
session of the twins, which made Laura slightly anxious in spite of knowing the babies were in good
hands.

Before the minister appeared, Laura whispered,
"You have a very nice family."

"Yeah, I like 'em. Most days." He leaned forward
to pick up a hymnal, opening it to the first song.

Laura suspected Eric more than liked his siblings
and his extended family. As an only child with a limited number of aunts and uncles, none of whom lived
in Helena where she'd grown up, she'd always envied
families like his. They seemed to make their own fun.
That was probably why both Laura and her mother
had been so welcoming of Amy.

Not that her far smaller family unit hadn't had fun,
too. Sunday mornings roughhousing with her dad and
reading the comics together were memories she'd always cherish. There simply weren't as many people
in her family as other folks had.

Reverend McDuffy, with his white hair and folksy
way, provided his congregation with a blessedly short
sermon, perhaps because of the shrill duet Rebecca
and Amanda began shortly after he started to speak.

As the congregation stood, Laura plucked Becky
from Kristi's arms. Eric claimed Mandy. Together

they slipped out a side door and found a quiet bench behind the church where they could feed the babies.

"For such tiny things, they sure have big lungs," Eric commented.

"Future opera stars," Laura suggested. "Although their harmony is a bit jarring."

He grinned and plugged a bottle into Mandy's mouth.

Sitting companionably on the bench, the babies sucking on their bottles as though they hadn't eaten in days, Laura leaned back and relaxed. Big Sky Country was putting on a show today. In the distance, a line of dark, black clouds bisected the wide swath of cerulean sky, and the hazy outline of the Glacier Park mountains was barely visible. Closer at hand, redtail hawks spiraled upward, catching the lift from the warming earth. In between, prairie grass shimmered silver and green in an almost imperceptible breeze.

"This is nice," she said on a sigh.

"Yeah."

"Can't think why Grass Valley doesn't get more tourists."

"Maybe because we don't want them."

She cocked an eyebrow. "Good point."

The hum of a dragonfly's wings and the call of a mockingbird filled the silence. It was all Laura could do to remember that this peaceful interlude only masked reality. This moment wasn't hers to keep. Just as the twins weren't Eric's to keep, unless she said so.

Odd how that one thought carried with it so much regret.

A few minutes later, Lizzie found them, announcing that the potluck and baby shower were about to get underway.

VIRTUALLY THE ENTIRE congregation stayed for the potluck, and most of them brought at least a small present for the twins. The adults sat in a circle on folding chairs, the more agile ones on the floor, during the gift-opening process, while the younger children played outside under the supervision of a mother or two. The teenagers lounged around outside, too, ogling each other, giggling and generally acting like adolescents do everywhere in the world.

Not that it was any of her business, but Laura surreptitiously glanced around the room. There seemed to be no single women between the ages of twenty and thirty, no marital prospects for Eric. To her dismay, she was pleased with that observation, and her reaction wasn't entirely due to the threat that his finding a bride would mean she might have to give up the twins.

It had far more to do with her own totally inappropriate, no doubt unwelcome attraction to the man.

Shaking away that errant thought, Laura opened the first package, a small box with a big, pink bow from Marlene Huhn. Inside she found two bibs with the twins' names beautifully hand embroidered on them, making the bibs almost too nice to use.

"These are exquisite. Thank you," Laura said.

One gift led to another and then another. There were crib sheets and blankets, dolls and rattles, handmade wooden pull toys the twins wouldn't be able to use for ages, but still much appreciated.

Doc Justine gave her a book on what to expect in a baby's first year of life. "Most babies come up with something those authors didn't think about, so you give me a call when they do. We'll take a look."

"Thank you. I will." She flipped through the pages, a little overwhelmed by it all. She had a similar book at home but hadn't thought to bring it. She passed this one to Eric. If the babies stayed with him, he'd need it.

Trying not to think about that possibility, she continued unwrapping presents.

Valery Haywood had crocheted two sweet little sweaters, one with a fuzzy poodle and the other with a kitty on it.

The gift from Hetty Moore was even more welcome.

"A double Snugli carrier," Laura exclaimed as she opened the box. "Wherever did you find it?"

"We get enough catalogs at the store every day to fill a barn. Took me a while to find what I was looking for, but there you are." Hetty beamed with pleasure.

"Thank you so much. It's…everything is so wonderful. And thoughtful."

Laura was touched that these men and women, who were strangers to her and the twins, would go to so much effort for them. But perhaps the gifts were just another example of the love and support Eric had in the community. They wanted him to keep the babies, not Laura.

She wasn't quite that quick to be persuaded, however. In this case, it took more than a village to raise a child.

As the grand finale, Kristi rolled out a tandem stroller, and everyone oohed and aahed.

"The family went in together on this one," she said. "Granted, we don't have a whole lot of sidewalks in Grass Valley but we got the model with the bigger wheels so it would go better on gravel and dirt."

"It's wonderful," Laura said. There were miles of paved walking paths in her townhouse complex and around the neighborhood. Eric's family hadn't thought about that.

Eric plucked Rebecca from Valery's arms—she was about the tenth woman who had cuddled her in the past hour—and put the baby in the stroller. "Whadaya think, Tinkerbell? Shall we let your sister try out her seat, too?"

With a happy squeal, Becky let her approval be known.

By the time the shower was over, and everyone had had their fill of potluck, the twins were exhausted from overstimulation and Eric needed help carrying all the gifts to the truck.

When Laura put Mandy into her car seat, she was crying hard and wouldn't take her pacifier. "It's all right, sweetie, you're just tired. Mommy will have you home in a few minutes and in your own bed so you can have a nice, long nap."

Eric's hands froze on the stroller he was folding to put in the back of the SUV. He hadn't heard Laura call herself Mommy before, but the word had sounded as natural as putting thick cream on strawberries.

She wanted to be the twins' mother. She'd made no secret of that. And maybe she even deserved it, since she and her mother had given Amy a home when his sister had needed a safe place to be. Laura would probably be a damn good mother, too.

But the twins belonged with family. That meant him. For the life of him, he didn't see any room for compromise on that issue.

Besides, it had been less than a week and he'd already bonded—if that's what you call it—with the twins. He loved them. Even in the middle of the night when their cries dragged him out of bed, he loved the way they snuggled into his arms and looked up at him with complete trust. He'd never be able to walk away from them. Or let them be taken from him.

As he finished folding the stroller, stuffed it inside and lowered the SUV's hatch, he wondered how any parent could.

He also knew it wouldn't be easy for Laura to give them up.

SINCE HE HADN'T BEEN PAGED all day while at the church, Eric assumed law and order prevailed in Grass Valley. Therefore, discovering that the three messages on his answering machine at home had nothing to do with breaking the law didn't surprise him. Which didn't make him all that thrilled with the messages.

He found Laura collapsed on the couch after putting the twins down for their nap. Her head was tipped back, her eyes closed, and there were dozens of unwrapped presents piled on the floor they hadn't had a chance to put away. A tiny frown marred her smooth forehead, and he had an almost irresistible urge to kiss that frown away.

Instead, he shoved his hands in jean pockets and cleared his throat.

She opened her eyes, as blue as a Montana sky, and Eric got another jolt. Clearly he'd been celibate too long.

"I had some phone messages while we were gone," he said. "It seems one of my brothers placed a personal ad in a couple of newspapers."

Her brows arched. "A couple?"

"Two or three." Helena. Great Falls. Boise, Idaho. God, what had they been thinking?

"Impressive."

"The newspapers printed some pretty flattering things about me." Mostly lies, Eric decided. Certainly exaggerations. "We may get a few women dropping by in the next few days. To meet me."

"I see."

Well, hell! She could at least react to the possibility he'd actually find a wife. He wasn't all that bad a catch. He had a good job, a house. Money in the bank.

"I just wanted you to know," he said.

"I'll try to stay out of your way."

"I'll make sure, if I pick one of them, that they'll be a good mother for the twins."

"And I promise to represent Amy's wishes as best I can."

He heard her unstated threat. *It's in my hands!*

The phone rang.

When he didn't move, Laura cocked her head toward the kitchen. "You'd better answer that. She could be the one."

Eric scowled and stalked toward the kitchen. This whole deal of needing a wife was totally unreasonable. Laura ought to see that. He was capable of raising the twins on his own. In Grass Valley, he'd have plenty of help. Besides, he didn't want to be forced into marriage to anyone.

He snatched up the phone. "Eric Oakes."

"Is, uh, Laura Cavendish there?" a male voice asked.

Well, if that didn't just beat all! "I'll get her."

He marched back into the living room. "It's for you."

She looked up in surprise. "My mother?"

"Not unless she has a bad case of laryngitis. I'd say it was a guy."

"Oh." With a little shake of her head, which shifted her hair across the delicate line of her jaw, she pushed up to her feet. "I can't imagine…"

Yeah, sure, like she was pulling one over on Eric. She had a boyfriend. So what? It didn't mean the guy would end up Becky and Mandy's dad. Eric was first in line for that job.

He paced around the living room until Laura returned.

"That was the superintendent of my school district, Alex Thurman," she said.

All the steam Eric had built up over the unfairness of his situation with the twins blew away. "On Sunday night? He wields a mean whip."

"Not really." She seemed agitated, picking up one of the gift boxes they hadn't yet put away, looking at the contents, then setting it aside. "I mentioned to you the curriculum coordinator's job I applied for. He just offered it to me."

"Congratulations."

"The problem is he wants me back in town by the first of the month."

"That's only a week away."

"I'll need to get things set up before classes start in late August, so the teachers can prepare."

Eric could understand that. But what about the twins' future? Where did they fit in?

He still needed a chance to prove he was the father they needed.

And find a wife.

A week didn't give him much time.

Chapter Six

The first of Eric's wannabe brides from the personal ads showed up early the next morning.

"Bernice Zeidlitz here," she said, extending her hand when he opened the front door. "My friends call me Bernie. You must be Eric Oakes."

"Uh, yes." She pumped his arm as he tried to blink the sleep from his eyes. It was a little after eight, and the twins had alternated being awake last night, which meant Eric had gotten little sleep himself.

Scanning him up and down like a piece of meat hanging in a cold-storage locker room, she said, "You'll do, I suppose. Reasonable physique for a civilian, but I don't like seeing men half-naked. Proper attire is important for morale."

His or hers? Rubbing his hand across his bare chest, he figured she was lucky he'd bothered to pull on his pants. The woman was on the stocky side, closer to forty than thirty and wore her blond hair in a short, no-nonsense style. But Eric wasn't in a position to be picky about who he married. He wasn't looking for a lovefest, just somebody who was good with babies. "I was sleeping. We had a hard night with the—"

She marched past him into the living room. "Sounds like we'll have some trouble adjusting to each other's biorhythms. I'm a morning person. Up with the dawn, that's my motto. 'Reveille' was my favorite time of the day at boot camp."

"Boot camp?"

"Right." She did a smart about-face and stood at parade rest. "Marine drill sergeant, recently retired. I'm ready to settle down to a home and family now. This seems like as good a place as any."

Good God! "There are a few things we need to discuss before—"

"Where are these new recruits you've got? The twins?"

"They're upstairs sleeping. As I said, it was a long—"

"Sleeping? At this hour? We can't have that. Need to get them on a proper schedule." She headed for the stairs. "Up at six. Breakfast from six to six forty-five. Then playtime."

"Now, wait a minute." He took off after her, but she was quick, apparently in great physical shape, and got to the second floor before he did.

"Which way?" she asked.

"Let's wait until they wake up, then you can meet them when they're at their best." Unless he could get rid of her first.

"I always say, begin as you plan to continue. Might as well get the little darlings started on their schedule now."

Laura appeared in her doorway, pulling on her robe and looking suitably rumpled from their exhausting night.

Bernice halted abruptly.

"Who are you going to put on a schedule?" Laura asked, running her fingers through her sleep-mussed hair.

"More to the point, who are you?" Bernice wanted to know. She shot an accusing glance toward Eric. "I have no interest in being a part of a ménage à trois."

Nor did Eric. "Laura Cavendish meet Bernice Zeidlitz, marine drill sergeant, retired. She came in response to the personal ad in the paper."

Laura's lips tightened, her eyes narrowed. "I see."

"Drove most of the night to get here," Bernice announced. "Wanted to be first in line, so to speak. Don't believe in that old military saw of not volunteering for anything. But it looks like you outmaneuvered me and hit the beach first."

"No, that's not—"

Eric took Bernice's arm, trying to ease her back downstairs. From the feel of her biceps, short of tossing her over his shoulder, he suspected she'd budge only if she wanted to.

"How about I fix you a cup of coffee?" he offered in lieu of a wrestling match, which he wasn't all that sure he'd win. "You've had a long drive. It's the least I can do."

She hesitated long enough that Eric wondered if she were planning to overwhelm Laura and establish her own beachhead right here in the upstairs hallway.

"How 'bout you point me in the direction of the

kitchen? I'll get the coffee started while you finish putting on the uniform of the day.''

''Perfect. Downstairs and around to your right.''

''Hope you like your coffee high-octane. That's not an area where I'm willing to compromise.'' With a quick nod as her salute, she paraded past him to the stairway, head held high, back ramrod straight.

She was barely out of sight when Laura said a sharp, ''No.''

''That makes it unanimous.'' He gave her a weary smile. ''I'll get rid of her as soon as I can.''

''Thank you.'' Anger laced her taut response, which was in direct contrast to her sleep-rumpled appearance.

Eric liked her softer side, the way she looked in the night holding one of the twins, her drowsy smile when the baby went back to sleep. It was the kind of smile that made him want to cuddle her in his arms, hold her spooned against his body as they lay in bed waiting for sleep to come. Except he figured he'd want to do more than just snuggle together.

Which wasn't on the agenda for either of them. She had a job to go back to, a boss who wanted her there in a hurry. Eric was fighting her for custody of the twins. Hopping into bed together didn't seem like a good plan. Not that his libido was in full agreement with that decision, particularly at a moment like this when both of them were only half-dressed. And the alternative of sleeping with Sergeant Zeidlitz gave him the chills.

As though reading his thoughts, she tugged her robe more securely around her. ''Instead of giving your address to every woman who calls, maybe you ought to do a little prescreening on the phone.''

''Good idea. I'll be sure to check if they have any objections to seeing a man's bare chest.''

Laura's brows shot up. ''She doesn't like your chest?''

''Apparently half-naked men offend her sensibilities.''

She sputtered a laugh. ''And here I was thinking what a really nice chest you have.''

''You were?''

''Muscled but not too hairy.'' The hint of a blush colored her cheeks, and she glanced away, shrugging. ''I'm not fond of hairy.''

''I didn't know women noticed one way or the other.''

''Oh, yes, they do.'' A tiny smile teased at the corners of her lips. ''Men's chests provide endless hours of conversation in college dorm rooms, for instance.''

''I thought it was only guys who talked about—''

''Oakes!'' Bernice bellowed from downstairs. ''Where do you keep your coffee?''

Eric held up his hand to Laura. ''I'll get back to you on that list after I get rid of Sergeant Zeidlitz.'' He ducked into his room to grab a shirt, and as he did he heard Laura's soft chuckle behind him.

In spite of himself, he smiled in response. *She likes my chest.*

LAURA HURRIED to take a quick shower while the babies were still sleeping and Eric was dealing with the latest would-be bride. At least this woman hadn't raised an iota of jealousy on Laura's part. Her reaction was closer to anger that someone would try to take over the entire household, including *her* babies, without so much as a by-your-leave.

Good grief, somebody should have made that woman a general!

Besides, how on earth could any woman not like looking at Eric's chest? Or anything else about him, for that matter. His reluctant smile—when he deigned to use it—brought a twinkle to his clear blue eyes. His broad shoulders looked capable enough to take on a world of burdens. Even from the rear view, his buns in tight jeans were worth admiring.

And Bernice didn't like his bare chest? Unbelievable.

Laura sighed as the water pelted her body, and wished she could linger in the caressing warmth. She hadn't had a chance to indulge in a long, leisurely shower in months. Not since the birth of the twins. If she retained custody it would probably be years before she had that opportunity again.

A price she was more than willing to pay, she reminded herself.

Stepping out of the shower, she toweled off and ran a quick comb through her hair. One of the advantages of a two-parent family was the chance to take turns caring for their babies. A nice arrangement for those who could work it out, and exactly what Amy had wanted for her twins.

Which meant if Eric found a suitable wife, Laura would have to relinquish the twins to him…and a stranger.

A sharp pain sliced close to her heart. Tears stung her eyes.

If she were *whole,* capable of producing children of her own, she might have found a man to love years ago, one who could love her in return. But life had dealt her a hand that was one card short of a full house. Since her accident she had felt the emptiness in her womb as though it were a cavernous pit devoid of hope.

Becky and Mandy had filled that hole in her life. To give them away would break her heart.

By the time she'd dressed, the twins were cooing in their crib, conversing in a language only they could understand. Laura imagined the two of them would always share a special link that would grow stronger over the years. She desperately hoped she'd be there to see it.

She changed their diapers, adding her own nonsense syllables to the conversation, and carried them both downstairs. The aroma of black coffee was so strong it gave her a caffeine jolt simply by inhaling the scent.

She peered cautiously into the kitchen. Eric was sitting alone at the table, a coffee mug in front of him.

"Is she gone?"

He glanced up and smiled. "Marched off into the sunrise whistling the theme from *Bridge over the River Kwai.*"

"Oh, dear." She laughed.

"Yeah." Holding out his hands, he said, "Let me have one."

"You can have both. I'll fix their bottles."

"Watch out for the coffee. It'll grow hair where you really don't want it growing."

"Thanks for the warning."

He took the babies, adjusting one in each arm as she went to the refrigerator to get the bottles she'd mixed last night. Over the past few days she'd grown comfortable in Eric's kitchen. The appliances might not be the newest, the counter was tile rather than a more modern granite, but it had a workable layout. A family kitchen that only needed a woman's touch to make it a home.

"In a way I feel sorry for her," Laura said. She put the bottles in the microwave and punched in the time.

"For the sergeant? I don't think she's looking for sympathy."

"Hmm, maybe not. But every woman deserves to find love somewhere." With the microwave humming, she leaned back against the counter. The twins were completely content in Eric's arms, looking up at him as though he'd painted the moon especially for them.

"I doubt the recruits she trained had a lot of love for her. She is one tough lady."

"All the more reason why she's looking for love now." Which made her and Bernice sisters of the heart, even if Laura wouldn't trust the woman to raise the twins. Raising children required far more flexibility than molding marines into a fighting force.

The microwave dinged. She retrieved the bottles, screwed on the tops, gave them each a good shake, then tested them for temperature with a few drops of formula on her wrist.

"I think you're right about making a list," Eric said.

"Oh?"

"Bring me a pad of paper and a pencil from the drawer over there." He gestured with a nod of his head. "We'll do it together."

Great. She was going to tell him exactly who he needed to marry so he could get custody of the twins. Talk about being her own worst enemy!

Between them they got everything arranged, each with a baby and bottle, the pad and pencil in front of Eric, Laura sitting opposite him at the table. The twins latched on to their respective bottles; Laura and Eric got to work.

"She has to be good with babies," Eric said. He had Becky's bottle propped under his chin while he wrote that down on the paper. "How about being experienced with babies?"

"That would be a plus," Laura conceded. "But remember, most new parents aren't experienced. I certainly wasn't but I've managed pretty well."

"Yeah, you have. We'll give experience bonus points. What else?"

"After Bernice, maybe we ought to say flexible."

He grinned at Laura and wrote that down. "Got it."

She was at a loss what else a mother needed to be successful. "Love of the twins seems like it ought to be the primary ingredient."

"That's a given."

"She's going to be your wife. Don't you have any ideas?"

He pondered that for a moment. "Good-looking?"

"It figures a man would think of that first."

"I don't mean she has to look like a fashion model. But if we're going to...you know... If you were planning to get married, wouldn't you want your husband to be decent-looking?"

"If he loved me and was good to the twins, I wouldn't care what he looked like."

"Except for the hairy-chest part."

Her sharp laughter startled Becky, and the infant's eyes flew open. Laura brushed a quick kiss to the baby's forehead to soothe her.

"Sense of humor." Eric wrote it on the list. "That's important in a wife."

"In a husband, too."

Their eyes met and held, sending a warm quiver of awareness burrowing into Laura's midsection. The air in the kitchen grew heated, as though the oven had been switched on or the day had turned excessively warm.

"Intelligent," he said softly, his gaze still focused on her.

"You like intelligent women?"

"You can't spend all your time, uh, in bed. I like a good conversationalist. Besides, when the twins are older, she'll have to help them with their homework and stuff."

"You won't?"

"Sure, but I wasn't all that good at English and history. Math was easier."

"History is my specialty. When I was young, I spent so much time at the library reading musty old books, they threatened to charge my parents rent. Now I try to teach kids what's happening today is tomorrow's history."

His lips twitched with a smile. "There was a girl in high school—Emily Trudough. She let me read over her shoulder during history tests. Without her, I never would have gotten through the French Revolution."

"Tony Eaton got me through geometry."

"Guess that means we don't have to put down honesty as a criteria."

She laughed again. "Juvenile crimes of the minor sort can be excused, I suppose."

They discussed a dozen other issues. Since he lived in a small town, the would-be bride had to be comfortable with that. Liking the outdoors was important, too. Montana had more of that than anything else.

Hobbies were considered but they didn't seem to matter to Eric as long as they didn't include skin piercing or yodeling.

There was one question she didn't want to ask. The answer seemed all to obvious. But a man ought to give some thought to his answer before choosing a wife, as she knew all too well.

"What about more children?" she asked, her throat tightening in anticipation of his answer.

He wiped some dribble from Mandy's lips with the corner of clean cloth diaper and glanced up. "Sure. I've always wanted a big family. Maybe not four adolescent boys at once like Walker has but big enough for some roughhousing. When you're dumped like I was as a kid, you think a lot about family. How important it is. From what you've said, Amy was probably the same way.''

''Yes, she was.'' Which is why Laura had been sent off on this fool's errand, risking the chance she wouldn't be able to keep the twins for herself.

But giving Eric—or any other man—the family he longed for wasn't in the cards for her.

In that regard, she'd never measure up.

AFTER A SIMPLE BREAKFAST, Eric went to the office, and Laura tried to do some laundry. Not only had a load of dirty baby clothes piled up, she had all of the shower gifts to take care of before the twins could use them.

Apparently the twins had a different idea about how she would spend her day.

They wouldn't nap for more than twenty minutes at a time. They woke crying as though the end of the world were about to arrive. They weren't hungry and wouldn't take their pacifiers.

Laura was at her wits' end and frantic with worry. Eric had been called out somewhere. He probably wouldn't have known what to do any more than she did, and she'd read through the entire baby-care book without finding a solution to their crying.

Out of desperation, she called Doc Justine at the medical clinic across the road, about a block away.

Kristi answered and listened to Laura's concerns.

''Bring them right over. It may be nothing to worry about but we'll take a look at them.''

Rather than take the time to put the car seats back into her car, Laura used the new dual Snugli carrier for the twins and walked the short distance to the clinic. Normally she would have enjoyed the brisk walk. The day was gloriously sunny, the temperature in the seventies. Wildflowers dotted the open fields. But she was simply too distraught and harried for this to be a pleasurable stroll.

Naturally the twins thought it was a wonderful outing. They both dozed right off to sleep, the rocking motion as she walked—and their obvious fatigue— lulling them into giving up the battle to stay awake.

The clinic was in an old Victorian house with dormer windows and a wide front porch. A little bell jingled as Laura opened the door and stepped inside. Glass-topped display cases filled with antique medical equipment lined the entry hall, and the faint scent of antiseptic laced the air.

Kristi appeared from a room on the left, looking crisp and professional in her turquoise medical jacket. "Hi, Laura. Your little bundles not bringing much joy today, huh?" She brushed her palm over Mandy's head in a quick caress that probably gave her an instant gage of the infant's temperature.

"Right now they're being angels. But they were awake half the night, and they've been fretful all afternoon. I couldn't get them to sleep—until now."

Doc Justine arrived from the opposite side of the house. "Let's get double-trouble into an exam room where we can take a look." Barely pausing beside Laura and the babies, the doctor strode across the hall and toward the examination rooms.

Laura followed. "Now that they're finally asleep, I hate to wake them up."

"Unless you want to learn how to sleep standing up yourself," Doc Justine said, "we'd better find out what's wrong and fix it."

Laura shot a troubled glance at Kristi.

"Don't mind my grandmother," she said. "Med schools didn't teach bedside manner when she attended, but she knows what she's doing."

"Humph! Never cured anybody of anything with sweet talk." Despite her crusty bearing, the doctor lifted Becky from the Snugli carrier as gently as a light breeze would lift a feather.

Kristi did the same with Mandy.

Both babies began to squirm as their temperatures were taken, hearts listened to, ears and bottoms examined, all with a minimum of wasted motion.

Finally the doctor announced, "Fine, healthy babies, both of them."

"Then why are they so fussy?" Laura asked, a new wave of desperation washing over her. She dreaded the thought of another sleepless night.

"Go ahead and tell her, Kristi," the doctor ordered.

"It looks like teething to me."

Astonished, Laura looked back to the doctor for confirmation. "Teething? They're only three months old."

"More like sore gums, actually. Nothing to worry about." Doc Justine unhooked her stethoscope from around her neck and draped it over a wall peg. "Used to be we'd say a baby that teethed early was extra-smart. Course that isn't true, but it gave the mothers some comfort."

"But what do I do?" Suddenly Laura felt helpless, ill prepared for motherhood. She'd never considered teething or sore gums to be the problem, though perhaps she should have.

"Used to be we'd have the mother rub a little whiskey on the baby's gums to ease the pain."

"Whiskey?" Laura gasped.

"Near as I can recall, the whiskey was more a comfort to the mother when she took a nip or two off the bottle herself."

Laura sputtered an objection.

"Grandma, will you stop baiting her." Shaking her head, Kristi finished dressing Becky. "I'll call Harold over at the pharmacy and have him pull some numbing gel off the shelves. Just rub a little on their gums every few hours as needed. They'll sleep better, and in a day or two the gums will stop hurting."

"I certainly hope so." Laura tugged Mandy's shirt back on and hooked her tiny overall straps in place. The baby was crying so hard now, tears welled in her eyes. "Oh, sweetie, I'm so sorry your mommy didn't know what to do."

Doc Justine's hand closed over Laura's shoulder, squeezing gently. "You and Eric are doing a fine job with these babies. They're as healthy as can be. They're lucky to have parents like the two of you."

Tears stung Laura's eyes, too. She and Eric *couldn't* be the twins' parents, not at the same time, at any rate. And not for the long haul. One of them was going to lose custody. Laura was desperately afraid she'd be the one, and the strain was beginning to tell.

ERIC RETURNED HOME about dinnertime. He found the twins sleeping peacefully in the playpen near the window in the living room, Laura curled up on the couch equally out of it, her hands pillowing her head. A huge pile of unfolded laundry filled the overstuffed chair by the fireplace. There had been no sign of dinner preparations in the kitchen as he passed through.

Given everyone's sleepless night, he suspected Laura had collapsed from exhaustion. He didn't blame her in the least.

She stirred, stretching her legs. Her mouth worked but she didn't speak. During the course of the day, she'd worn off her lipstick, leaving her lips a natural shade of rose and all the more inviting because she was so guileless.

Eric wondered how she would react if he kissed her the rest of the way awake.

He hunkered down beside her. Tempted, he teased the tips of her ginger-blond hair with his fingertips. Silky. Lush and thick. The kind of hair a man wanted to thread his fingers through as he kissed a woman senseless.

Her eyes blinked open, sky blue and filled with surprise. Or maybe it was pleasure.

"Hey, Sleeping Beauty." His voice was hushed, his throat tight. "You have a hard day?"

"Mmm, you could say that."

He focused on her mouth. If he leaned forward a

few inches, his lips would be on hers. "You want to tell me about it?"

She studied him with quiet intensity. "The twins were so fussy I finally took them to see Doc Justine. It's nothing serious," she hastened to add. "Sore gums. She had me get some numbing gel at the pharmacy."

Relieved the babies were okay, Eric relaxed from his momentary fright. "You did the right thing, taking them to see the doc, I mean."

"When I went to get the gel, the pharmacist practically forced a two-scoop chocolate ice-cream cone on me." A tiny furrow formed between her brows. "He didn't let me pay for it, either."

"Harold's quite a character. He rarely lets his customers decide what kind of ice cream they'd like. He makes the decision for them, and he must have thought you needed an extra pick-me-up."

Her lazy, contented smile agreed with Eric's assessment. "Nothing has ever tasted so good."

"I'm glad." Unable to help himself, he brushed a few strands of hair back from her face, then rested his hand on her downy-soft cheek.

A sigh shuddered through her. "How was your day?"

"Routine." There'd been a gas station robbery in a neighboring town, and he'd been alerted. But it wasn't his jurisdiction so he wasn't the primary investigator. Just back-up this time. In rural counties, they helped each other.

"You must be tired, too. You didn't get any more sleep last night than I did."

"I'm okay." He liked being right where he was. Close to her where he could catch her feminine scent, a combination of baby powder and the sweet perfume of a woman.

Her eyes opened wider. "Oh, my gosh! I haven't even started dinner."

"There's no rush. In fact, why don't I take you out to dinner?"

"Out?" She echoed the word as though he'd spoken in a foreign language.

"Yeah. We can go to the saloon in town. They've got pretty good burgers and sandwiches. A couple of decent salads, if you'd rather eat light. Nothing fancy, of course."

"You don't know how tempting that sounds."

She was tempting, too. The vee of her blouse collar opened just enough to reveal the swell of her breast as she took each breath. The smooth curve of her hip was within his reach. Her soft, sensual lips...

"But what about the twins?" she asked, her voice still rusty with sleep, her eyes as deep as velvet. "Do you think it would be all right to take them?"

"Sure. We could put them in their car seats right in one of the booths with us. They'd probably love all the activity." He would enjoy a different kind of action, one of a far more intimate nature.

"All right. Let's do it."

For a moment he thought she'd agreed to do what he'd been so vividly imagining, and his body reacted with a powerful ache. The two of them together, right there on the couch, caressing, stroking, exploring with hands and lips and tongue.

And then one of the twins awoke, babbling little cooing sounds. Laura levered herself to a sitting position, gave Eric a wistful smile, and the moment passed.

He sat back on his haunches. He didn't know whether to thank little Becky or curse the infant's bad timing because he wasn't quite sure what was happening between him and Laura.

Or what would happen if he pursued the matter.

Would she just be another woman who walked away from him?

Chapter Seven

The jukebox blared a hard rock number, a twirling spotlight spun overhead, and the saloon smelled of stale beer. The floors were darkly stained and worn from years of use. The vinyl seats in the booth had long since lost their spring.

The twins loved the place.

So did Laura, more because she was sitting across the table from Eric than because of the ambience.

He'd almost kissed her. She could hardly believe it was true.

She'd felt his warm breath on her lips, sensed his desire. In response, heat had gathered in her midsection, stealing her breath. Her nipples tightened and a heaviness weighted her limbs that she hadn't experienced in years. All because he had looked at her that way.

And then Becky had done her thing. Darn it all!

She reached for the menu, her hand trembling with residual frustration.

Eric leaned forward across the table. "Take a look at the two guys at the bar and tell me what you think."

"What?"

"What do you think they're doing here?"

Trying not to be conspicuous, she glanced over her shoulder.

Dressed in khaki pants and sports shirts, the two men were drinking beer, and it looked like they'd each had a hamburger and fries. Both in their late twenties, one man was a good fifty pounds over-weight, and he straddled his bar stool as though it were a horse. The other guy was lean, with stringy brown hair that hadn't been cut in a year. Neither wore cowboy boots like every other male in the saloon, Eric included. He'd changed into jeans and a denim shirt, rolled the cuffs up and looked like he was a working ranch hand come into town for a bite to eat. Not a cop.

She turned back to him. "Not locals."

"Tourists?"

"I wouldn't think so. More like hunters taking some time off from their wives, but it's not hunting season."

"Then why are they in Grass Valley?"

She frowned and decided to reverse the tables on him. "Why are you so curious about them?"

"Well, for one thing there was a gas station robbery in the next county this afternoon. For another, I spotted an unfamiliar pickup with a shell in front of the saloon. We don't get much out-of-town traffic. Makes me wonder."

She loved the way a police officer's mind worked, filled with curiosity and always asking questions. They noticed things no one else would. Her father had been like that until he died—a heart attack at far too young an age. She'd always felt she'd been at fault for his premature death. If she hadn't insisted on that wild joyride in the back of the pickup.

"So what do you think?" she asked, pressing away the memory along with the guilt. "Robbery suspects?"

"Neither one fits the description of the perp. But eyewitnesses can be pretty far off the mark."

"I suppose." She glanced at Becky, gave her a smile and tickled her tummy. That circling light overhead had her enthralled.

The bartender finally showed up to take their order.

"Hey, Sheriff. How's it going?"

"Can't complain or you won't vote for me next time."

The young man grinned, barely old enough to vote, Laura suspected.

"Laura, meet Stitch Overholt. He's got a spread out east of town and is moonlighting here 'cuz his wife's expecting their first."

The young man glanced at the babies in their car seats. "Sure hope we only get one at a time. I don't know what I'd do with two."

"I'm sure you and your wife would manage," Laura told him.

"Yes, ma'am." He flushed a beautiful shade of pink. "What can I get you two?"

"First, what can you tell me about those two at the bar?" Eric asked. "Have they been in before?"

The kid thought a minute. "I seen the heavy-set guy a couple of weeks ago."

"Either of them say what brought them to town?"

"Nope. Not that I can recall. Probably just passing through."

Nodding, Eric glanced at Laura. "What did you decide to have?"

She recognized the signal to not ask any more questions, and looked up at the young man. "The Cobb salad and whatever you have on draft."

Eric's head snapped up. "A beer?"

"I had a hard day, remember?"

He grinned at her. "Since I'm not in uniform, I'll have a double burger, fries and the same as the lady to drink."

"Yes, sir. If it's okay to say so, Sheriff, your wife's real pretty."

Heat scalded Laura's cheeks. "I'm not—"

"You've got a good eye, Stitch. But you'd better get back to work before I decide you're hitting on the wrong woman."

"Yes, sir." He backed away from the table and all but ran back to the kitchen to place their order.

"I'm sorry," Laura said. "I thought we'd stopped people from thinking—"

"Don't worry about it. Stitch just hasn't gotten the word yet." His thoughts had clearly shifted back to the two men at the bar. Not tourists, yet passing through, one of them for the second time.

Obviously Laura and the twins took a back seat when he had law enforcement on his mind.

So much for their *almost* kiss.

THEY WERE PUTTING the twins down for the night when Eric's office line rang. He hurried across the hall from the nursery and answered the phone in his bedroom.

Minutes later he reappeared, dressed in his uniform and wearing his gun on his hip.

"I've got to go out," he announced.

Disappointment shot through Laura. "Now?" What a ridiculous question. Of course he had to go. He was the local sheriff. He gets a call and he has to respond. Whatever had she been thinking...or hoping for?

"Another gas station robbery. They appear to be moving west."

"The same perp?"

"Same MO."

"Our guys from the saloon?"

"It's possible. This time the attendant spotted a pickup with a shell on the back when the perp fled. He had an accomplice." He bent over the crib to kiss the twins good-night. "I passed on the license number of the pair that was at the saloon."

He stood up just as she was bending over to straighten the crib sheet, and they collided. He grabbed her by the shoulders to steady her, which brought their bodies in contact from shoulders to hips, her breasts brushing against his chest.

For a breathless moment they stood there, uncertainty and desire mixing in the air, overwhelming the scent of baby powder. Laura's heart pumped hard, as though she'd run up a dozen flights of stairs. She was trapped. A part of her wanted to run, to avoid the heartbreak that even a single kiss would lead to. Another part of her demanded that she take what she could. Drawn like a hummingbird to the promise of sweet nectar, she leaned forward.

Instead of meeting her mouth with his, Eric's hands slid down her arms in a slow caress until he was holding both of her hands. "Sorry," he whispered.

Sorry? That he didn't want to kiss her? Dear God! Was there anything more foolish than an overeager woman?

"I really have to go."

"I understand." In her self-delusion, she'd read the signs all wrong.

"I don't know how late I'll be."

With what was left of her pride, she lifted her chin. "That's all right. The twins and I will be fine."

A slight frown furrowed his forehead, and he released her hands. "I'll see you in the morning, then."

Unable to speak past the lump in her throat, she nodded.

"There's a woman planning to stop by tomorrow. Delores Haghan. She called about the ad. Sounded like a possible over the phone."

Disappointment, sharp and painful, left her standing in the nursery as Eric walked out. She heard his footsteps descending the stairs, then the back door open and close. Only then did she let the tears come.

How many times did she have to learn the same lesson? She wasn't worthy of a man's love.

By MORNING Laura had her emotions back under control, blaming the whole incident on what turned out to be PMS. That was the cruelest joke of all. Her hormones could go on a rampage like any other woman's but she'd never be able to deliver the goods—a baby of her own.

When one door closed, she reminded herself, another one opened. The twins were her solace, her joy. A consolation prize she intended to cherish. Eric Oakes would have to come up with a whale of a good prospect for a wife before she would even consider relinquishing the babies to him.

And he'd need to do it in a hurry. Both for the sake of her heart and her career, Laura couldn't remain in Grass Valley much longer. She needed to accept that job Alex Thurman had offered her and get on with her life.

With Becky in her arms and Mandy in her car seat, Laura was feeding the twins when Eric came into the kitchen for breakfast.

"Good morning." He went to the bread box, took a couple of slices and dropped them in the toaster before pouring himself a mug of the coffee she'd fixed. "Once I got home last night, I must have crashed pretty hard. I didn't hear the babies at all."

"I thought you'd be tired, so I let you sleep. The twins were good, though." She kissed Becky's forehead. "They slept four hours straight and only woke up once, at three. And went right back down again after I put some of that gel on their gums."

"Boy, that sounds like progress, doesn't it?"

She stiffened her resolve. "Yes. But last night does illustrate the problem of my even considering giving custody of the twins to you."

"How so?"

"Eric, you get called out to work at irregular hours. Unless you have a wife—"

"I'm working on it."

"I'm aware of that. Under some circumstances a live-in housekeeper might do. But I'm not willing to agree to an arrangement like that. A housekeeper is too likely to move away or want to get a better job."

The toast popped up but he ignored it. "In a pinch I could take the twins to Rory's place. Nobody's more qualified to take care of babies than Kristi is."

"The point I'm trying to make is that the twins deserve a consistent caregiver. A real *mother* figure. It's what Amy specifically wanted, and I'm not convinced you can provide that."

"You promised to give me some time."

"Time's running out, Eric. I've got to get back to Helena. I have my own life to think about."

"So you're saying you'll never have an emergency? Not even a late-night meeting you have to attend?"

"Not on my new job. And if I do, my mother lives only ten minutes away. She won't be a stranger to the twins but someone they are familiar with and already love."

He yanked the toast from the toaster and spread butter on the cold bread. "Sounds like you've already made up your mind what you're going to do."

"Not entirely. You said there's a woman coming today."

"Great. If she's not satisfactory in your view, I lose, huh?"

She hated herself for agreeing with his assessment, but that was about the size of things. "I'll be happy for you to be a part of the twins' life. You're their uncle. We can keep in touch. You can come visit."

"Forget it, Cavendish. I plan to fight you for the twins. In court, if I have to. Family counts."

She opened her mouth to speak but snapped it shut when the doorbell rang. The next wannabe bride applicant? Her stomach did a tumble.

Before he turned to leave the kitchen, Eric sent her a look that said he'd never give up.

Stubborn man! Why couldn't he have been content with being a loving uncle? In a child's world, that was an important role. Why did he insist on being their father when Laura wanted so much to be their mother?

She lifted Becky to her shoulder, gave her a little pat on the back, eliciting an unladylike burp. Then she switched the babies around, holding Mandy as she finished her bottle.

From the living room, she heard feminine laughter and Eric's deeper response. She grimaced at the good time they seemed to be having. Dear heaven, they'd only just met. What could they be laughing about?

Holding the woman by the hand, Eric brought her into the kitchen. She appeared to be about thirty with long, brunette hair and wide brown eyes that were striking in their intelligence and good humor. Her figure was equally well endowed.

Eric introduced them. "Delores, meet Laura Cavendish. She was a good friend to my sister."

Very poised, Delores crossed the room and extended her hand. "Call me DeeDee, please. And I'm honored to meet you. From what Eric told me yesterday on the phone, I can't imagine having a better friend than you were to his sister." Her eyes strayed to Mandy, and she smiled without a hint of guile.

"Nice to meet you, too," Laura said, straining to be polite. "Amy and I were more than friends. We were like sisters."

Sitting down at the table, DeeDee gazed with obvious longing at the twins. "What about the biological father? He'd have rights—"

"He's never been in the picture," Eric stated unequivocally. "From what Laura has told me about the way he treated Amy, he wouldn't get a warm reception if he showed up around here."

DeeDee glanced up at him, smiled, and looked back at the twins. "They're three months old?"

"A little more than that now," Laura said.

"This next year is going to be so exciting. They'll grow so fast and learn so much."

"You know about raising babies?"

Her bright, happy expression filled with sorrow. "I lost my husband and our two-year-old son five years ago in an accident. I never read the personals, really I don't. But for some reason I spotted Eric's ad." As though she couldn't help herself, she trailed a loving finger along Becky's cheek. "It seemed to reach out, as though it was written just for me."

Laura swallowed hard. She had no idea how any woman could recover from the loss of both a child and her husband. "I'm sorry."

"I checked out the accident," Eric said. "A multicar crash on Interstate 90. A big rig jackknifed. More than a dozen vehicles were involved, five deaths including DeeDee's husband and son."

Laura's stomach knotted.

DeeDee glanced toward Eric and then included Laura. "Please don't think I'm trying to duplicate the family I had. I know I can't do that. But it's time I moved on with my life and well…'' Very gently, as if she were testing the water in an unfamiliar swimming pool, she lifted Becky from the car seat. ''If I had a chance to love these two precious babies, I'd feel like I'd fulfilled my life.'' She glanced over her shoulder, her smile hopeful. ''I'd be a good wife, too, Eric. I promise.''

For a moment Laura wanted to snatch the baby back from DeeDee. The woman had no right to hold *her* child—the baby she loved. But that wasn't true. If Eric had found an appropriate wife for him and a good mother for the twins, Laura had to accept that. It's what Amy had wanted.

Her lungs nearly closed down tight. Who in their right mind would expect her to give up the twins to someone else when she had the power to say no?

Except the nagging voice of her conscience told her she wouldn't have any other choice. Not if it was the right thing to do.

They'd all visited for a while in the kitchen, DeeDee getting acquainted with the twins. Eric had to admit it was damn uncomfortable, DeeDee talking like the babies were already hers to raise and Laura barely able to string two words together, she'd been so tense.

Not that he blamed her. She loved the twins, and DeeDee looked to be a serious contender to replace her as their mother.

Once they managed to get the babies down for their nap—sort of fumbling all over each other in the process, Eric decided to take DeeDee on a tour of the place. At least that would give Laura a few minutes of peace.

He walked DeeDee out to the corral. Both of his sorrel geldings trotted over to the fence to greet them.

"I only keep a couple of horses here," he said. "Mostly for recreation or if someone gets lost and we have to do a ground search."

"Oh, they're a handsome pair," DeeDee said. She stroked the muzzle of the first one who'd hung his head over the fence.

"That's Archy and the other one is Bashful."

She laughed. "I'm sorry I didn't think to bring apples or carrots for them."

"They're really looking for sugar cubes, but that's bad for them." Resting his arm on the top rail of the corral, he studied her while she petted the horses. Attractive. Certainly friendly. Nice figure. Laughs easily, which was saying something for a woman who'd lost her entire family not that many years ago. "Do you ride?"

"I haven't in years. My grandparents used to have a ranch not far from Jordan, which isn't actually close to anywhere. I spent some summers there as a kid."

"So you like small towns?"

"Absolutely. I loved being at Grandma's house and taking the big trip into Jordan on Saturday to do the shopping." Her smile was warm and engaging, filled with happy memories. "Great Falls is fine. And I have lots of friends there. But moving here wouldn't be a problem. Grass Valley looked quaint as I drove through."

Quaint wasn't exactly how Rory would describe the town—that sounded a little too high class, he thought. Like Swift Eagle was too ritzy sounding for Rory. He was just a guy. Eric's brother. Like Grass Valley was just a town.

"The one thing that does bother me," she confided, "is guns. Particularly around children."

He could understand that and echoed her concern. "At home I keep my weapon in a locked safe in the kitchen right by the back door. I never wear it inside the house. And my bigger artillery I keep at the office, also under lock and key."

She smiled at him softly. "You're a good man, Sheriff Oakes."

He sensed she was a good woman, too, and damned if he wasn't sorry there weren't any sexual sparks flying. He ought to be attracted to her. Everything about her seemed *right*.

Maybe when they got better acquainted...

He showed her his small barn, not that it was worth writing home about, but it served his purposes, and the detached garage where he housed his police vehicle at night. His tools were stashed there, too.

"I've got two acres here plus the house. I also have an interest in the Double O Ranch out east of town, but my brother runs that."

"A brother?" She cocked a brow in wry amusement. "You mean there are more like you somewhere?"

He felt heat color his cheeks. "Naw, I'm unique."

"I can see that, Eric. I really can."

Well, hell! He'd finally found a woman who thought he walked on water and he didn't get the charge he'd hoped for. He kept thinking about Laura inside the house, worried about what was happening, terrified she'd lose the twins.

Damn, life wasn't fair.

The day seemed to drag. He took DeeDee to the office. She seemed dutifully impressed with his job and the jail cells, and gratified they were unoccupied.

He took her to lunch at the saloon. Nobody commented, but he got an odd look from Joe Moore, who was sitting at the bar having a hamburger and a beer.

When they got back to Eric's house, DeeDee gave Becky her afternoon bottle and seemed to relish the experience. *Poignant* came to mind.

Distress registered in Laura's expression. But to her credit, she didn't say a word. She was one courageous lady because Eric knew how much she was hurting.

In Eric's head, a clock as giant as London's Big Ben kept ticking. He didn't have much time to choose a wife. Laura was planning to leave soon. She'd take the twins with her unless he could find a way to stop her.

After the twins went down for their nap, Laura stayed upstairs, claiming she had some paperwork to do for school.

Downstairs DeeDee stood in the middle of the living room, glancing around as though studying every angle, every nuance, branding them into her memory.

She exhaled deeply. "I think both of us have a great deal to think about."

"Yeah. That's true."

"I'm going to go back home now—"

"You could stay the night. The accommodations wouldn't be great but—"

"No. I'm going back to Great Falls." Slowly she

walked toward him, then stood on tiptoe, pressing a kiss to his lips. "You call me about your decision, okay?"

"Yeah, I will." He wanted to feel something. Anything! But the warmth of her lips didn't do squat for him. Or his libido. Why the hell not? She'd make a great mother for the twins but—

Palming his cheek, she smiled. "It's not there, is it?"

"I don't know. I mean—"

"It's okay. I loved my husband desperately. It was probably foolish of me to even think of this kind of marriage of convenience. But you have taught me something."

He frowned. "What's that?"

"That I am capable of caring about another man. I needed that lesson." Her smile was both sad and hopeful. "I'm going to use that lesson and move on with my life. Thanks."

"DeeDee, I—"

"No. From what I've seen, you ought to be taking a serious look at Laura."

"She loves the twins, but I'm not part of the package."

Cocking her head, she studied him a moment, then smiled. "Well, thanks for the grand tour. Keep me posted, huh?"

"Sure, I—"

She was out the front door before he had a chance to say anything else. Slipping into her two-door sedan, she gave a friendly wave as he stood rooted to the front porch. And then she was gone.

Desperation gnawing at his gut, Eric wondered

what to do next. He'd pretty well eliminated all the women who had called, and he hadn't had the courage to propose to the one applicant who had pretty well fit the bill. Laura had a job to go back to in Helena.

Behind him, he heard the screen door open and her footsteps on the porch.

"I thought DeeDee might stay for dinner. I was going to do a chicken casserole."

He didn't turn, couldn't bring himself to look at her. "She needed to get back home, to Great Falls."

"I see."

He whirled around. "No, you don't. She knew, dammit, that I wasn't going to propose to her. She matched every damn item on the list we made, but I wasn't going to pop the question." His breath drove hard and painful through his lungs.

Her frown lowered her brows. "Why not?"

"Because it wasn't fair to you, that's why not."

She shook her head. "I don't understand."

"You love the twins. So do I. Amy wanted them raised by both a mom and a dad." He didn't know why he hadn't throught of this before. Maybe DeeDee's comment had triggered the idea.

Maybe he should have considered the possibility earlier.

Shoving his fingers through his hair, he took a deep breath, almost as if he were planning to jump off a cliff into a deep pool of icy-cold water. "The only thing that makes sense here is if you and I raise them together. That the two of us get married."

Chapter Eight

Laura gaped at him, dumbfounded. Her heart was in her throat, her stomach had plummeted clear to her toes. Knees suddenly weak, she reached for the porch railing to steady herself.

"What are you saying?" Her voice was barely more than a whisper. Was he really proposing marriage? Or had her hearing been affected by too many sleepless nights? Or too many fantasies?

Folding his arms across his chest, he leaned back against the porch post. "It's the logical thing to do. Amy will get what she wanted, and we'll both get to raise the twins. We'll adopt them together."

Whatever was happening, this wasn't like any proposal Laura had dreamed of receiving. "Logical? For two people to marry who barely know each other?" Forget she was falling in love with Eric. That wasn't the issue. "You can't get married just for the sake of the children. That isn't at all logical."

"Why not? Couples *stay* married for their kids all the time. You wanted me to find a wife out of the

Live the emotion™

Anytime. Anywhere.

We'd like to send you 2 FREE BOOKS

and a surprise gift to introduce you to Harlequin American Romance®. Accept our special offer today and

Live the emotion™

HOW TO QUALIFY:

HOW TO QUALIFY:

1. With a coin, carefully scratch off the silver area on the card at right to see what we have for you—**2 FREE BOOKS** and a **FREE GIFT**—ALL YOURS! ALL **FREE!**

2. Send back the card and you'll receive two brand-new Harlequin American Romance® novels. These books have a cover price of $4.75 each in the U.S. and $5.75 each in Canada, but they are yours to keep absolutely free!

3. There's no catch. You're under no obligation to buy anything. We charge nothing—ZERO—for your first shipment and you don't have to make any minimum number of purchases—not even one!

4. The fact is, thousands of readers enjoy receiving books by mail from the Harlequin Reader Service® Program. They enjoy the convenience of home delivery…they like getting the best new novels at discount prices, BEFORE they're available in stores…and they love their *Heart to Heart* subscriber newsletter featuring author news, horoscopes, recipes, book reviews and much more!

5. We hope that after receiving your free books you'll want to remain a subscriber. But the choice is yours—to continue or cancel, any time at all. So why not take us up on our invitation with no risk of any kind. You'll be glad you did!

GET A *Free* MYSTERY GIFT…

We can't tell you what it is…but we're sure you'll like it! A FREE gift just for giving the Harlequin Reader Service® Program a try!

Visit us online at
www.eHarlequin.com

Your FREE Gifts include:

- 2 Harlequin American Romance® books!
- An exciting mystery gift!

blue. At least you and I have been living together for more than a week. We haven't come to blows yet.''

''That's hardly the same thing as being married.'' Separate bedrooms. They hadn't even kissed, not once, assuming close didn't count. Their most intimate moments had been during the middle of the night when they each had a lapful of baby.

Trying to regain her equilibrium, Laura sat down on one of the two wicker chairs on the porch. She couldn't agree to a marriage without love. The pain of living with Eric, being his wife, and knowing he didn't love her would be too much to bear. Eventually it would wear away at her self-respect and her patience. Her libido would either shrivel to nothing or spin helplessly out of control from overstimulation because Eric didn't desire her in the way she wanted him.

It wouldn't take long for others to realize their marriage was a farce. Even the twins, as they grew older, would recognize the absence of love.

She blinked back the tears of regret that flooded her eyes. ''No. I can't do that.''

Straightening, Eric jammed his hands in his pockets. She'd let him know exactly where he stood: at the end of the line in terms of a marriage prospect. DeeDee had been way off base about Laura wanting to give him the time of day. He tried not to feel disappointed. She hadn't come to Grass Valley looking for romance.

But he wasn't a man who gave up easily. And he wasn't going to lose the twins if he could help it.

"Okay, here's another idea," he said. When a rodeo bronc threw you, you tried again. Winners didn't quit. "A compromise. We can keep on as we are, you living here, taking care of the twins. A housekeeper-nanny arrangement."

Her eyes widened, then narrowed. "Eric, I have a job. A career. I'm about to be promoted. You can't expect me to simply give up—"

"We've got a school right here in town. Maybe not as big as the one you're used to or as fancy. It's a K-through-12 with about four hundred students. Small classes. Good academics. They're on summer break right now but I could take you over there. Let you take a look."

"You're suggesting I could teach, and in my spare time I can be your housekeeper and the twins' nanny? Do you have any idea how many hours a teacher works beyond the hours they spend in the classroom? It's a sixty-hour week."

Mentally throwing up his hands, he paced around the porch, his booted feet heavy on the old wooden planks. "You don't have to work at all. I'll pay you, whatever you want. I've got plenty of income to support you and the twins." He was getting desperate now, his options shrinking to none. "For God's sake, I don't know what else to suggest. I'm running out of ideas. You could give me some help here, okay? I'm trying to make this work for both of us."

She dipped her head, her blond hair sliding across her chin, forming an impenetrable veil of gold. "I know. But I don't think it's possible. Not the way you're proposing we do it.''

His jaw clenched on a curse. ''Makes me wonder if you ever intended to give me a chance with the twins. Maybe you planned all along to show up, tell me I didn't fit the bill and then scurry back to your own life.''

''That's not true. At least, not entirely.''

''Yeah, sure.'' He walked off the porch steps. Behind him the sun was lowering in the sky, casting long shadows, and the summer air was beginning to cool. In the distance the plains stretched out to the horizon, broken only by an occasional rise in the ground that could barely be called a hill.

He loved this country. It was his home, tough winters and blistering summers alike. Oliver Oakes had brought him here almost twenty years ago, and Eric had put his roots into the soil. He didn't want to move to Helena. He doubted, with the metal pin in his leg leftover from his rodeo days, the police force would hire him. So what kind of job could he get? Night security? Hell, that was no kind of job at all.

If it made any sense for him to go with her to Helena, he'd give it a shot. But it didn't.

On the porch, he heard the creak of the wicker chair as Laura stood. ''I'm sorry, Eric. I'm not sure what I expected when I came here, but I...I have to go home.''

''You're taking the twins?''

''I can't leave them. Not under the circumstances.''

He swore low and succinctly.

"If you don't mind," she said, "I'll stay the night, do some packing and leave in the morning. I don't want to disrupt the twins' schedule too much."

"Whatever." He shrugged, though it pulled shoulder muscles that were way too tense. She'd been perfectly willing to disrupt not only his schedule but his life. He almost...*almost* wished he hadn't learned about the twins. That he had a sister. That he was an uncle to his own flesh and blood.

It would be easier if he hadn't known.

FOR THE FIRST TIME since the twins were born, Laura was grateful for their penchant for being fussy during dinner. Between the racket and juggling babies from car seat to wind-up swing to someone's arms, conversation was impossible. She didn't know what to say to Eric, anyway.

Apparently he didn't, either. He looked so glum, he might well have just lost his best friend. In a way, she supposed that's what he was feeling. She was taking the twins away from him.

It was as though she were killing his sister—for a second time. And he'd only just learned that she had existed.

But what was she supposed to do? Of course men did raise babies on their own. Even adopt babies themselves. But that wasn't what Amy had wanted for the twins. And with the irregular hours that came with Eric's job, the logistics seemed insurmountable.

Even so, her conscience kept sitting on her shoulder, jabbering at her that there had to be another way.

She hated to hurt anyone. Eric was a good man. He'd make a wonderful father.

But she'd make a good mother, too. The twins were her only chance to prove that.

In her effort to do the right thing, she'd put both herself and Eric in an untenable position.

Getting up from the table, she cleared their plates. She noted Eric hadn't eaten much more than she had. Their respective appetites had apparently fled together.

"Why don't you leave all that?" he said, holding Becky to his shoulder and patting her back. "I'll get it done while you start your, uh, packing."

She swallowed hard. "Are you sure?"

Nodding, he shifted Becky to the other shoulder and reached over to give the swing another crank, setting Mandy in motion again. "I've got it covered."

"All right." The tension in the room was too thick, her conscience too prickly for her to want to linger.

Upstairs, she gazed around the nursery, not knowing quite where to begin. The twins had received so many gifts she'd need more than the one suitcase she'd brought to pack their things in now. And what should she do about the dual stroller? Eric's family had given them that. It didn't seem fair to haul that off to Helena.

Or the infant swing, which Eric had bought himself. And the oak dresser.

Maybe he could get his money back. The dresser, at least, he could use for other things.

She set out a couple of clean outfits for the twins

to wear in the morning. The bibs Marlene Huhn had hand embroidered were in the same drawer. Laura ran her fingertips over the carefully scripted names. She'd like to take the bibs with her—for the twins. They needed to have tangible evidence of their short stay with their uncle Eric.

Regret thickened in her throat as she placed the infant garments in the suitcase. If Eric had expressed any affection for her, she might have stayed with him. Agreed to be his wife and hope that someday his feelings for her would deepen.

Very likely that would have been a foolish dream. One that would hurt more acutely with each passing year.

Finally she'd squeezed everything she could into the twins' suitcase. She'd need a cardboard box or some grocery sacks in order to pack the rest of the toys and clothing. Eric would have to decide what he wanted to do with the larger gifts.

As she walked down the stairs, she heard Eric singing softly, his voice a mellow baritone. Her heart hitched when she realized it was a lullaby. He, or more likely his brothers, had been wrong about Eric not being able to carry a tune. He and Amy shared the same musical talent.

Tiptoeing into the living room, she found him with Mandy settled in the crook of his arm and Becky propped on his crossed knees. The sweet, haunting sound of his voice reached out to her even as it soothed the babies. The pain and desolation she heard tore at her heart.

Dear God! How could she do this to him? The elemental unfairness of their situation shattered what little self-control she'd been clinging to, and tears edged down her cheeks. Whatever was best for the twins had to be the right thing to do for all of them. If she suffered in some small measure as a result, it was a minor sacrifice to make for their happiness.

"I'll stay," she whispered.

Slowly Eric lifted his head, his eyes red-rimmed, questioning her.

"I've changed my mind," she said with a little more force. "I'll stay with you and the twins, if you still want me to."

He seemed to struggle to regain his composure. "Yeah. That would be fine. Good."

Impressing her with his enthusiasm didn't appear to be on his mind. "Not as your housekeeper, though. This is a pretty small town. If you and I live together, no matter what we said about our relationship, people will think that—"

"We're having sex."

"Yes." Her lips had gone as rough as toast, and she licked them. Not that it helped much. Her mouth was almost as parched as her lips. "I don't want the girls growing up thinking that we're doing anything...illicit."

"Then you're thinking we ought to get married?"

Actually, she was thinking she'd lost her mind. She'd turned down his proposal only hours ago and now she was asking him. In both cases, they were acting as though they were negotiating a contract that would barely change their lives. Like buying a car. Or taking out a loan for a vacation trip.

"I assume we're talking about a marriage-in-name-only," she said.

He eyed her a moment before speaking. "If that's what you'd like."

Love would be so much nicer. That wasn't one of the choices. "I think it's wiser that way, don't you? No emotional baggage. Just an arrangement."

Mandy had dozed off, and he tried to adjust her position. Laura hurried to pick her up. Her hand brushed against Eric's, warm masculine flesh against her cooler skin. A sensual current shot up her arm, speeding on its way to her midsection, and she nearly wept because that was all she'd ever experience with Eric—unfulfilled desire.

How in heaven's name would she avoid making a fool of herself for the rest of their married life when he affected her so strongly after only a week?

An easy trick to accomplish, she reminded herself, since he didn't appear to want her in the same way she'd begun to want him.

She slipped Mandy into her car seat on the floor as gently as possible so she wouldn't awaken.

"You do understand," she said, "that by marrying me—even if it weren't just an arrangement—that I'd never be able to give you the family you wanted. More children."

He glanced at Becky, asleep in his arms. "That won't be a problem."

"Fine, then." Contract agreed to. Shouldn't they

at least shake hands, she thought on the edge of hysteria. Fix their signatures to some multipage form? "I'll have to call my boss, let him know I can't accept the coordinator's job. Or even teach in the fall." She'd miss that. She truly loved cramming history into those rebellious teenage brains when they were barely aware it was happening. Or helping other teachers to do the same with their students.

"You want to teach here?" Eric asked. "I could talk to the principal, see if there are any openings."

"To tell you the truth, for the next year or so, maybe until they're in school, I think it would be better if I stayed home with the twins."

His lips twitched ever so slightly. "A full-time, stay-at-home mom?"

"Their first few years are crucial. If you can afford—"

"I can. And I like the idea." As gently as if he were handling a porcelain doll, he laid Becky on the couch beside him. "What do you want to do about the wedding?"

"Well, I..." She hadn't been thinking that far ahead. How should she act, what should she wear for a marriage ceremony that was no marriage at all? "Let's keep it small. Very low-key."

"I could arrange for a judge in Great Falls to marry us in his chambers."

"That will be fine," she agreed. She refused to mourn the loss of a church wedding in a white gown with friends and family hovering around her. Her marriage to Eric would not be a celebration.

"We'll need a license. And it may take a few days for the judge to clear his calendar."

"No problem. When we get the license, we can begin formalizing the adoption."

"Sounds reasonable. I'd like to have my brothers attend the wedding, if you don't mind. You could invite your mother."

Sitting on the floor beside Mandy, she fiddled with the pad in the car seat, straightening it. Trying to breathe past the pain in her chest.

"Since it's the only wedding I'm likely to have, I imagine inviting my mother would be a good idea. It's going to be hard enough on her as it is, moving the twins up here permanently. She'll miss them terribly."

"She can visit whenever she wants. Kids need a grandma, and I've got lots of room for her to stay here."

"I'll tell her. Thanks."

"It'll be your home, too. You can have anyone visit that you want to. You'll probably want to do some redecorating, too. As long as you don't go hog wild, anything you want is fine with me."

"There's the furniture at my condo." She glanced around, trying to imagine her lighter, more feminine taste contrasting with his masculine choice of leather and dark wood. "I'm afraid it won't go well with what you already have."

"Then we'll toss my stuff. Or move it into the den. I want you to feel comfortable here."

He was being so damn generous it hurt. But most of all, it hurt because he didn't love her.

What else could she expect? Gary Swanson, the one man she had been foolish enough to believe *could* love her, had made it clear she was less than the ideal mate. So be it. She'd devote her life instead to being the best mom possible.

With luck, she and Eric would become friends. Companions who put the best interests of the twins first. She didn't dare hope for more.

Glancing out the living room window, she noted twilight was beginning to settle in, leaving the cottonwood tree in the front yard in shadows. When they were old enough, the girls would love having a swing hanging from one of the big branches.

Her chin quivered. She'd look forward to giving them their first push.

AFTER SPENDING the next morning making arrangements for the wedding and starting the adoption ball rolling, Eric headed across the road to Rory's place. He was going to tell his brother about the upcoming nuptials and wished he felt better about the situation.

He'd practically forced Laura into agreeing to marry him. Backed her into a corner. She was so damn soft-hearted she hadn't been able to take the twins away from him. She'd sacrificed her home and her career for his sake and her own desire to be a mother. Not many women had that kind of courage or were that generous.

He wasn't sure what he could give her in return.

But he'd do his darnedest to make sure she was never sorry about her decision.

Five-year-old Adam was riding his two-wheeler in circles on the clinic driveway, his dog, Ruff, chasing him around and around. The dog peeled off from the game to greet Eric, his shaggy tail wagging like a semaphore flag. Of indiscriminate breeding, Ruff appeared to be mostly sheep dog, his eyes hidden behind long, uneven bangs.

"Hi, fella." He scratched Ruff behind his ears and patted his side, so thick with fur it was hard to tell where the dog ended and the fur began.

"Hi, Uncle Eric." Adam wheeled around and slid to a stop in front of Eric, sending gravel sailing from the ten-inch wheels.

"Hey, there, kid. I'm gonna have to ticket you for reckless driving if you keep this up." He knocked his knuckles on top of the boy's safety helmet.

"Uh-uh. I'm too little to get a ticket."

"Don't count on it, Little Gray Puppy. I'm a pretty tough cop, you know."

"Little Gray *Wolf!*" The youngster giggled, laughing at Eric's incorrect use of his Indian name, his dark eyes flashing. "You're not tough. You're my *uncle*."

He gave the boy's shoulder a squeeze. The twins would grow up knowing Adam and any of the boy's siblings who might come along. Walker's kids, too. They'd have lots of cousins to play with and watch out for them. They were lucky little girls—all because Laura had such an unselfish heart.

A stab of guilt reminded him that he'd taken advantage of that admirable trait. Somehow he had to make it up to her.

"Where's your dad?" he asked.

"He and mom are inside fixing up a raccoon with a hurt foot. Want me to show you how I can do a wheelie?"

"Maybe later, okay?"

Ruff followed Eric as far as the clinic door, then dashed back to rejoin his playmate. The circling began again.

Inside the clinic, stainless steel glistened in the examining room where Rory and Kristi were bending over a sleeping raccoon working their medical magic.

"I sure hope you got paid before you started that procedure," Eric commented. "Last I heard, insurance benefits for raccoons didn't pay real well."

Kristi smiled at him from the end of the table.

Without looking up, Rory said, "He's kind of an old guy. We figure if we fill out the forms right Medicare will pick up the tab."

"Great. My brother's committing a federal offense, probably a felony, right under my nose."

Kristi shook her head in amusement, and Eric's lips twitched. She was used to their bantering by now—even when it revolved around an anesthetized raccoon.

"I figure I'm safe from the long arm of the law. It's not your jurisdiction so you won't bother to lock me up. Besides, if you did, you'd have to feed me, and you can't afford my gourmet tastes." Rory finished stitching the injury, clipped the thread and glanced over his shoulder. "What's up?"

"Laura and I are going to get married."

"Eric!" Kristi shrieked. "That's wonderful! She seems like such a nice woman, and the twins are so beautiful."

"Yeah, well, it's not exactly—"

Rory said, "I thought you were going to pick one of the women who answered the newspaper ad."

"They didn't work out."

"When? When?" Kristi wanted to know. "Lizzie and I will have to have a shower for her. Oh, this is so exciting."

"We're getting married next Tuesday. Judge Cole's office in Great Falls."

Kristi's eyes widened, and she gaped at Eric.

"Wow," Rory muttered. "That's pretty quick."

"You can't possibly get married that soon," Kristi gasped. "Or in a *judge's* office, for heaven's sake. That wouldn't be fair to Laura. Whatever are you thinking?"

"It's what we decided," Eric insisted, frowning.

"If that's what they want, honey—"

"Nonsense." Kristi yanked off her latex gloves and dropped them into the trash can, then nailed Rory with a wifely look. "I remind you, Rory Oakes, that both you and Walker were married right here in the Grass Valley Church with Reverend McDuffy performing the ceremony. Eric and his bride deserve just as much. And I'll tell you, as a recent bride, that as terrified as I was that day, I wouldn't have traded that ceremony for all the tea in China. I'll hold those memories close to my heart for the rest of my life.''

A blush appeared beneath Rory's olive complexion. "Me, too, I guess. Though the honeymoon is what I remember best.''

Rolling her eyes, Kristi hooked her wrist on her waist and glared at Eric. "So that's settled. You're going to be married at the church.''

"I don't even know if McDuffy would be available next Tuesday. He might have something else on his schedule.''

"Fine. Pick another time when he is available and ask the reverend to perform the ceremony. Tuesday is way too soon, anyway. Laura is going to have to find a dress, probably have it altered. She'll need to order flowers and let her friends know about—''

"Laura doesn't want to make a big deal out of the wedding,'' Eric insisted, his temper rising. This whole arrangement was hard enough on both him and Laura as it was. He didn't want his sister-in-law sticking her nose into his business. "Neither of us wants to make a fuss.''

Kristi's eyes narrowed and she shook her head. "Maybe you don't want a big production, but I'm telling you every woman dreams about her wedding from the time she's old enough to know what a wedding is. Nowhere in that dream is she standing in front of a judge who is wearing a black robe. Trust me on this, Eric.''

"She's probably right, White Eyes,'' Rory said

with a shrug. "Unless there's some big crisis, waiting another week or so wouldn't hurt, would it?"

"I guess not. But the fact is, she seems happy enough with the judge thing. She may not want to drag out this whole ordeal."

"Men!" Kristi huffed. "You leave Laura to me and Lizzie." Standing on tiptoe, she brushed a sisterly kiss to Eric's cheek. "Congratulations, Eric. I'm sure you and Laura will be very happy together."

Left standing alone with Rory in the examining room after Kristi whizzed out the door, Eric shook his head. "Is she always like that?"

"You mean stubborn and willful?"

"Yeah. Something like that."

Rory grinned. "She's great, isn't she? A take-charge kind of gal."

Eric mentally groaned. Already this marriage business wasn't working out exactly as he had anticipated. He had the terrible feeling a woman who became a wife metamorphosed into someone quite different.

He didn't want that to happen to Laura. He liked her just fine the way she was.

Chapter Nine

"Yes, Mother, I know it's sudden." Twisting the long, curling phone cord around her finger, Laura paced across the kitchen. The twins were down for their afternoon nap. It had seemed like a good time to break the news of the wedding plans to her mother. Or rather, Laura had decided there was no sense in putting off the inevitable.

"You barely know the man, dear." A rare hint of censure slipped into Barbara Cavendish's voice. "I think you ought to take some time—"

"He's as fine a man as I've ever met, Mother. And he loves the twins as much as I do." Only one small element was missing that would make theirs a match made in heaven—Eric didn't love her.

"But what about the wedding itself? I'd always hoped we could have a nice affair, nothing lavish, of course, but something where we could invite—"

"I'll be just as married this way. Eric and I have discussed—"

There was a knock on the back door and it opened. "Hello? Anybody here?" Kristi poked her head inside, grinning like a schoolgirl who had just learned the biggest secret in town. "Oh, there you are."

"Mom, I've got company. I'll call you back, okay?"

"I just wish—" Barbara sighed. "All right, honey. I'll talk to you later."

Lizzie followed Kristi into the kitchen. "Sorry if we interrupted you," Lizzie said with her usual gracious manner.

"I was talking to my mother."

Exuberantly Lizzie wrapped her arms around Laura, hugging her. "I hope your mom is as excited as we are. Eric just told us that you're getting married. Welcome to the family."

"We all wish you both the very best," Lizzie said.

"Thank you. I know it's a little sudden—"

"You've got that darn straight, sister." Laughing, Kristi led Laura to the table and sat her down. "There is no possible way we can get everything done by next week."

"Done? There's really nothing to—"

"You have to buy a gown. Even the fastest alterations take a week or more."

"I have a nice summer suit at home," Laura protested. "I thought I'd wear that." She'd ask her mother to bring it to the courthouse. Which meant she'd have to change in a stark public restroom, she realized with a shudder of dismay.

Lizzie sat opposite Laura at the table. "I think Kristi has something else in mind."

"In addition to getting you a gown, we need enough time to pull together a shower for you."

"Absolutely not. You've already given the twins—"

Kristi waved off her objection. "Furthermore, there's no way you want to be in a position that Lizzie and I can lord it over you twenty years from now that we were married in a church and you were married in some blah judge's chambers, for heaven's sake. So the judge thing is out."

Beyond confused, Laura stared at her future sisters-in-law. "You're not the kind of people who would—"

"Of course we're not now. But who knows what we'll be like when we hit menopause. You need to protect yourself."

Lizzie made a choking sound that was somewhere between a cough and a laugh, quite indelicate for her usually sophisticated manners.

"Now, as I see it," Kristi explained, "a trip to Great Falls is in order for the three of us. We'll help you pick out a gown—"

"She may not want to spend the money," Lizzie warned. "A formal gown can be pretty expensive for something you only wear once."

"Well, that's easy. She can borrow mine," Kristi volunteered. "Or yours," she suggested to Lizzie. "All three of us are about the same size."

"I didn't actually wear a gown when I married Walker—though I admit I arrived in Grass Valley with a gown in the trunk of my car that was suitable for a cathedral wedding.'' She smiled at the memory. ''I decided on something a little less ostentatious when the time came.''

Laura spoke up. ''I appreciate you're both trying to help—''

''Whatever you decide,'' Kristi insisted, ''you've got to have your own veil. I mean, the twins will want to wear that when they get married, don't you think?''

Tears suddenly welled up in Laura's eyes. She'd never been a weepy person, but the strain of the past ten days plus the approach of a loveless marriage had sent her emotions over the brink. Picturing Becky or Mandy at their own wedding coming down the aisle wearing the same veil she had worn to marry Eric was more than she could handle.

She covered her mouth with her hand as the tears crept down her cheeks.

Kristi patted her hand. ''There, you see? You'll need your own veil. We'll fix you up with tons of borrowed stuff, won't we Lizzie?''

''I have a pearl necklace my grandmother passed down to me that you're welcome to borrow. I did wear that for my wedding.''

''I'm sure Eric would want you to wear one of those frilly blue garters...so he can remove it,'' Lizzie finished with a grin.

''No, I really don't think—''

''Now, the reception.'' Kristi hopped up, found a notepad by the telephone and a pencil. ''Obviously there's nowhere decent in Grass Valley to hold a sit-down dinner, and I'm not fond of a potluck for a wedding reception. But I had a cake and punch reception, and Harold at the pharmacy furnished ice cream.''

"Which Fridge consumed in copious quantities," Lizzie added.

"Yes, well…"

Kristi was writing everything down. "Do you want to do printed invitations or drop notes to your friends? I could do up something simple on the computer, unless you'd rather go a little more formal."

"Formal won't be necessary."

"Lizzie, would you check with the minister about his calendar? See if he's got a Saturday open early next month. I get the feeling Laura and Eric are eager to get things going here."

Her head spinning, Laura said, "I really need to talk with Eric about this. We'd agreed—"

"I've already talked with that brother-in-law of ours. He'll agree to whatever we decide."

"Have you and Eric discussed a honeymoon?" Lizzie asked.

Laura flushed. In their case there wouldn't be a need for a honeymoon because they wouldn't be indulging in the intimacies that were usually involved. "No honeymoon." When both women looked at her in astonishment, she quickly added, "We can't leave the twins."

"Oh, we absolutely insist that you *do* leave the twins. A husband and wife need at least one night without interruption."

Lizzie nodded vigorously. "I'll second that. In fact, I'd recommend a week or more."

"Rory and I will baby-sit the twins," Kristi volunteered. "He needs to practice being around babies just in case, huh?" Her Cheshire grin suggested an ulterior motive behind her offer.

Laura made an attempt to gain some control over the wedding plans. But dealing with Kristi was like being caught up in a tornado; the wind took everything in its path.

She turned to Lizzie. "Is she always like this?"

"I think it comes from years of ordering people to use a bedpan."

Laura choked on a laugh. This whole wedding business was too much for her to deal with. If Eric wanted to object to Kristi's plans, he'd have to do it himself. She simply didn't have the strength to argue in the face of her own precarious emotions. Tears were far too close to the surface whenever she thought of the future and how she would survive a loveless marriage.

And the fact was, she would like something nicer than a simple ceremony in a judge's chambers. This was an event she didn't plan to repeat.

"You're right, ladies." Her quiet, determined voice halted their steamroller of ideas, much like a teacher silencing a classroom of rowdy youngsters. "Eric and I will be married in the church, and I'm going to wear a dress and a veil, just like I've always dreamed of doing. Eric will simply have to get used to it."

Kristi's gentle smile and her touch on Laura's hand told her that she'd made the right decision.

ERIC SCOOPED UP SOME OATS for his horses, handed a bucket to Laura and carried his to Bashful's stall while she fed Archy. It was well after dinnertime and the twins were down for the night, or at least for a few hours. Somehow in the past couple of weeks, chores had slipped to the end of his list of things to do.

"I'm going to have to get a couple of Walker's boys over here to exercise my horses," he said, giving Bashful an affectionate slap on his haunches. "I haven't had a chance to ride them since you and the twins have been here."

"The twins do consume a lot of time."

"Twice as much as one baby, I imagine."

"I don't know. I suspect babies simply fill up all the available time no matter how many there are. It's their nature."

"Yeah." For a woman mostly raised in the city, she looked comfortable around a horse, running her hand over Archy's mane, scratching behind his ears. Funny, he'd asked DeeDee right off if she liked to ride. He'd never bothered to ask Laura. Now it didn't matter. Either way, they were getting married.

God, he hoped this marriage was the right thing to do, not only for him and the twins but for Laura, too. She was giving up her home, her life, a career she was good at. He didn't want her to suffer for her sacrifice.

"Kristi and Lizzie came by this afternoon while you were out," she said.

"I thought they might. When Kristi gets a bit in her mouth, there's no stopping her."

Laura stepped out of Archy's stall, latching the door behind her. "They think we ought to get married at the church here in town."

"I already arranged things with Judge Cole."

"I know. And it's up to you, really."

He heard the hesitation in her voice and a hint of longing. "Is that what you'd like to do? Get married here?"

"It still wouldn't be anything fancy. Just family. But a judge's chambers seems so—"

"Cold. I know."

"It's the only wedding I'll ever have."

He swallowed hard. "Then we'll do it in the church." She deserved that and more for giving up so much. "You pick the date."

"I suspect by now Kristi already has." Laura's amused smile spoke volumes about what a good person she was. "I doubt I'll have to plan a thing. Including the honeymoon, if we let her have her way."

"Uh, honeymoon?" He hadn't thought that far ahead and wasn't sure he ought to, considering what a honeymoon usually entailed. Their in-name-only marriage wouldn't last long if he did.

"I told Kristi we couldn't leave because of the twins."

"That's true. It wouldn't be much of a honeymoon with a couple of babies along."

"She said she and Rory would baby-sit."

"Oh." He shoved his hands into his hip pockets as the image of Laura naked and beneath him popped into his head. His jeans grew snug at the thought, and he dropped his hands to his side, fisting his fingers.

"Under the circumstances we don't have to go anywhere. But people might think it's a little odd if we don't take at least one day."

The *night* was what he was thinking about. "Sure. We can do that. For appearances' sake, I mean."

"All right. You can make whatever arrangements you think will be suitable." Her gaze darted around the barn as though she was unable to look at him. "I'd better go back inside. I don't like to leave the twins alone too long."

"Fine. I'll be along in a few minutes." As soon as his libido cooled down a little. Maybe after a quick dip in the water trough.

After she left the barn, Eric leaned against Bashful's stall, exhaling slowly. How the hell was he going to keep his hands off Laura during their *honeymoon*, for God's sake?

He gritted his teeth. One night was going to seem like an eternity.

THE FOLLOWING DAY they drove into Great Falls to get the marriage license and sign the formal papers to jointly adopt the twins. Two days after that Laura opened the front door to a tall, slender woman with salt-and-pepper hair who appeared to be in her sixties. She carried a briefcase in her hand.

"Hello, I'm Mabel Cannery from Children's Services."

"Oh?" Laura felt a moment of panic. Why would Children's Services come to see her?

The woman's smile was reassuring. "You must be Ms. Cavendish. You and Eric Oakes filed to adopt Amanda and Rebecca Thorne."

"Yes, come in. Please." Assuming this was a routine follow-up to the papers she and Eric had filed, Laura opened the door wider and stepped back out of the way. Glancing around, she mentally groaned at the toys and blankets scattered across the living room. If only she'd had a little warning. She hurried to pick up some of the debris.

"Please don't worry about the mess," Mabel said. "If there weren't some clutter around, then I'd worry." She headed directly for the twins, who were in their playpen by the window. "What beautiful little girls."

"Yes, they are."

"Is Eric around?"

"He's at his office. I can call—"

"No, that's all right. I'll stop by to see him. This is only a preliminary home visit, and he and I are old friends."

"You are?"

"Between his father, Oliver Oakes, and more recently Walker, the Oakes family has pretty well kept me employed for the past twenty-some years."

"You were involved with Eric's adoption?"

"I was. And Walker and Rory." She glanced down

at the babies again. "They seem to have established a family tradition, adopting children."

"Eric is actually the twins' uncle."

"Yes, that was indicated in the adoption papers." She placed her briefcase on the coffee table and popped it open, removing a file folder. "I was wondering about the twins' biological father."

"I have no idea who he is."

"Generally speaking, a good-faith effort to locate the father is required in situations like this."

"I don't think he'd be at all interested in exerting his parental rights. He made no effort to contact Amy, their mother, at any time during her pregnancy or in the months since."

"I understand. The birth certificates indicate father unknown. Did Ms. Thorne know the father?"

Laura bristled slightly. "She didn't reveal that information to me. Her specific wishes were—"

"Yes, I have a copy of her request. And I understand you are currently the twins' legal guardian."

"Is there going to be a problem?"

"I wouldn't think so. I'm confident Eric will be a fine father, and you certainly appear well qualified. I simply wanted to clarify the situation."

"Of course." Becky was starting to squirm and fuss, so Laura picked her up. "Eric and I plan to marry soon. We'll provide the best home possible for the twins." Certainly better than their abusive father could, even if he were interested.

"I'm sure you will." She made a few notes in the file, then put it back in the briefcase. "I'll stop by to see Eric. I have to take some papers out to the Double O for Walker and Elizabeth to sign, so I'm actually killing two birds with one stone on this trip.'' She smiled and chuckled softly. ''Not that the county will appreciate how efficient I'm being by saving the mileage expense for a second trip.''

''I'm sure the taxpayers, at least, will appreciate your efforts, Ms. Cannery.''

She brushed a hand over the back of Becky's head and glanced again at Mandy in the playpen. ''I'd say these two are very lucky little girls. Thank you for seeing me, Ms. Cavendish. I wish you all happiness.''

Laura saw the social worker out as far as the porch, exhaling as the woman drove toward Eric's office. She didn't even like to think of the twins' biological father, much less consider he'd want to be involved in raising them.

Surely the issue would never arise.

MOST WOMEN HAD MONTHS to plan a wedding. Laura had had less than two weeks. Although Kristi had been such a whirlwind, there'd been little left for Laura to do.

She'd taken a day to meet her mother in Great Falls to shop for a dress—an ankle-length white dress that was a little too formal for Grass Valley but she hadn't been able to resist the scalloped lace neckline and empire waist that emphasized her bust. Deep in her heart, she knew the reason she'd succumbed to the temptation of the dress. She wanted to impress Eric.

She sighed at her foolish impulse.

"Are you all right, dear?" her mother asked.

They were in Reverend McDuffy's office waiting for the ceremony to begin. The groom was somewhere in the building, but Laura hadn't seen him since last night when his brothers had dragged him off for one last bachelor's fling.

"All brides are a little nervous, aren't they, Mother?" Though Laura had more reason than most to feel anxious. She'd actually been so afraid Eric would change his mind at the last minute that she hadn't finished dressing until he arrived at the church.

"I suppose. But this has all been so rushed." Looking worried, Barbara Cavendish fussed with Laura's veil, adjusting it at her shoulders. "Did you really fall in love with Eric in such a short time?"

The lump in Laura's throat was so painful, she could barely swallow. Tears stung her eyes. "Yes," she whispered, unable to find her voice.

"Then everything will be fine. And you know…" Her mother's eyes glistened, too. "I think Amy would be very happy that she had a part in bringing you and her brother together."

"I hope so. I really do."

"Your father would be so pleased, too. He wanted so much for—"

"Oh, Mom." Unconcerned about mussing her dress, she embraced her mother, holding her tight. "I've always felt guilty about Dad dying like that. If he hadn't been on duty and the one to respond to that stupid accident I was in and find me all mangled—"

"Laura Cavendish, don't you think for a minute

that your father's heart attack was your fault. I had no idea that for all these years—'' Barbara stroked her daughter's cheek, brushing away a tear. ''Don't you remember that Grandpa Cavendish died at an even younger age than your father did. Whatever was wrong with your father's heart, it was genetic. You had no part in his death.''

''But if he hadn't been the one to—''

''Hush. Today is *your* day. Donald wouldn't want you shedding tears over him today. More than anything else in the world, he wanted you to be happy.''

''I know, Mom.''

She sniffed. ''Then do exactly as your father would want. Enjoy every moment of your wedding.''

''I'll try.'' Although if her marriage to Eric had been based on love, not the desire to provide a home for Amy's twins, Laura would be much happier. ''Mother, would you walk me down the aisle? That way, Dad will be with us both.''

Her mother looked shaken by the suggestion but nodded. ''I think he'd like that idea.''

The office door opened, and Kristi poked her head inside. ''Everything's ready for you.''

Laura drew a deep breath and picked up the spray of cut flowers she would carry down the aisle. This is what she wanted—for herself and for the twins. Eric would be a wonderful father. A good many women would have settled for less.

Her courage almost faltered at the entrance to the small church. The small gathering of close friends and family members she'd hoped for nearly filled the chapel. The townspeople were present to add their blessings to the ceremony.

She took Barbara's arm, as much to steady herself as to honor both her mother and her father. The organist switched songs, and together they stepped forward. In a way, she felt her father's presence, too, and tried to force a smile. For him. For the love they had shared and the guilt she'd carried for so long about his death.

Her heart thundered in her ears so loudly she could barely hear the music as she walked down the aisle. Her mouth was dry and the flowers she carried shook as though caught by a sudden draft coming through the open doors.

Concentrating on taking one step at a time, she finally looked up and saw Eric waiting for her, handsome and elegant in a Western-cut pale-blue suit and bolo tie. Her breath snagged in her lungs at the smile on his face, the admiring look in his eyes. Hope surged through her as she walked toward him. For whatever reasons they'd been brought together, their marriage *could* work.

She vowed to do her part—from this day forward.

With a nod of acknowledgement to Eric, her mother left her side to take her place in the front row of pews, and the marriage service began.

The preacher's words were a blur as she clandestinely watched Eric from the corner of her eye. What was he thinking? That he'd been forced by her into this marriage in order to raise the twins he'd come to love? Despite the hope she harbored for their future, would he come to hate her for what she'd done? Granted, he'd been the one to first suggest marriage. But that didn't mean he might have preferred some other choice which included the twins but not her.

He was an honorable man. She knew that was true. He'd respect their vows but at what cost to him? He'd never find the perfect woman, his own true love, as his brothers had. It all seemed so unfair, what she'd done to him. Or perhaps what they'd done to each other.

Suddenly she felt Eric slip a gold band over her finger. She had a moment of regret that she hadn't gotten Eric a ring, too, just before Reverend McDuffy said, "I now pronounce you husband and wife. You may kiss the bride."

Startled from her musings, she looked up at Eric. They'd never kissed before. Not once. They'd come close. She'd certainly thought about kissing him. But never once had that fantasy come true.

One corner of his lips hitched into a half smile. "Maybe we should have practiced this part before we had an audience," he said softly for her ears only.

Before she could respond, he bent his head and captured her lips with his. Tentatively. Asking permission. His fingers lightly caressing her cheek.

A sigh of welcome, of recognition, trembled across her lips. Her heart wanted to believe this was right. That marriage was meant to be. The feel of him, the shape of his lips, their warmth, was familiar to her, as though in some other life they had been lovers.

The scent of his spicy aftershave was twenty-first century but her response was as ancient as time itself.

For a fanciful moment she thought of all the famous lovers who had filled the books she so loved to read—Romeo and Juliet, Antony and Cleopatra, Eliza Doolittle and Henry Higgins. She and Eric were none of those and yet they were the same.

Her heart was pounding hard when he broke the kiss, and she had no idea how long they'd been standing there in front of the congregation as husband and wife. Seconds or hours, it was as though time had stood still.

A ripple of applause circled the audience. One of his brothers said, ''Way to go, White Eyes!'' And Laura felt heat race to her cheeks.

Eric winked at her, turned them to face the crowd and they walked down the aisle together, her hand tucked in his arm.

Sometime later, while everyone was enjoying their fill of cake and ice cream, Rory came over, nudging her with his elbow and giving Eric a knowing look.

''You gotta watch out for this guy tonight,'' Rory said, nodding toward his brother. ''I'm told our sheriff likes to play with handcuffs.''

She sputtered, almost spilling her punch. ''Thanks for the warning. I'll keep that in mind.''

Indeed, after their kiss at the altar, their one allotted night for a honeymoon was very much on her mind. Handcuffs, however, had not been part of the image.

And then she recalled all too clearly that she'd been the one to insist on a marriage-in-name-only.

Eric was a man who played by the rules. Unless she did something drastic, he wasn't likely to change her decree.

Worse, despite the warmth of his kiss, he might not want to.

Chapter Ten

Laura got out of the SUV and stood beneath the pines, inhaling the sweet scent of the forest southeast of Great Falls. In front of her was a rustic ski lodge constructed of the same pines, a long porch stretching across the front of the building. In late August, no snow had fallen yet. Few cars were in the parking lot.

"This is lovely," she said. An idyllic spot for a honeymoon, remote and peaceful. Romantic. But perfect only if the marriage was to be a real one.

"Rory told me about the place. He and Kristi spent a few days here in June after they got married." Walking to the back of the truck, he lifted the hatch and hefted their two small suitcases out. He'd changed into jeans and a polo shirt at the church; she'd switched from her wedding gown to slacks and a blouse.

He stopped beside the truck, studying her and she felt her forehead furrow. "You were pretty quiet the whole drive. Are you okay?"

Not really. "I miss the twins," she said, hedging. "I haven't been away from them for a whole night since I brought them home from the hospital.'' While that was true, being away from the twins wasn't Laura's biggest concern at the moment. Her *honeymoon* was.

''Then you deserve a night off. All mothers do now and then. Kristi and Rory will take good care of them.'' He cocked his head toward the lodge.

The nervous flutter in Laura's stomach that had plagued her since their kiss at the altar picked up velocity as she walked up the porch steps beside him. They'd left the reception early and made the trip here in little more than four hours. Now, as the sun dipped behind the mountain ridge, waning columns of sunlight danced through the tops of the trees, turning the pine needles to silver.

At the knotty-pine registration desk, a bright young woman wearing a white shirt with the lodge's logo on the pocket greeted them with a warm smile.

''Good evening. You must be Mr. and Mrs. Oakes.''

Laura's stomach took another dip. *Mrs. Oakes.* How long would it take her to get used to her new name?

As though he did this sort of thing every day, Eric signed the register for them both while she fidgeted with the shiny gold band on her finger. A sure giveaway that they were newlyweds.

The young woman passed him the key. ''The honeymoon suite is through those doors and to the left. Room five. Dinner is served until nine o'clock, and breakfast is available starting at six. The suite has a hot tub. It's *very* private,'' she emphasized with a knowing smile.

''Thanks.''

''I didn't bring a swimsuit,'' Laura whispered as they walked away from the front desk.

He canted her a wicked smile. ''I think the young lady was making the point that we won't *need* a swimsuit.''

''Apparently I forgot to mention that I'm the modest type.''

''I'm not.''

They went out the back and followed the decking around to room five. He slipped the key into the lock and pushed open the door, holding it for her.

She hesitated at the threshold. ''Maybe we should have gotten separate rooms.'' At opposite ends of the lodge, she thought a little hysterically.

''We'll manage with one.''

Having a good many second thoughts about their *arrangement*, she took a shaky breath and stepped inside.

There was nothing rustic about the huge bed that filled one end of the room or the cozy love seat in front of a native rock fireplace. A sliding glass door beside the fireplace led onto a small porch and provided a view of the grassy ski slopes beyond the lodge. On the opposite side of the room the enclosed hot tub was clearly visible through another glass door.

Thus far she'd only seen Eric naked from the waist up. But it didn't take much imagination to picture the rest of him—narrow hips and long, muscular legs lightly covered with sandy-brown hair. His manhood nestled in a thatch of the same color hair.

She blinked, trying to rid herself of that image but to no avail.

"This is great." he said, placing her suitcase on a stand in the walk-in closet. "No wonder Rory has such fond memories of his honeymoon."

"It's possible he was remembering Kristi more than the accommodations."

"Yeah, I guess he would." He strolled around the room, testing the bed, opening drawers in the low dresser, peering outside. "Well, what do you want to do? Eat dinner or take a dip in the hot tub first?"

"Dinner," she blurted out, though she wasn't in the least hungry. Her nerves were too on edge to eat a bite. But that was better than the alternative of getting naked in a hot tub with Eric.

Her gaze slipped to the bed. No matter how large it was, sleeping with him wasn't a good plan, either. And she doubted either of them would be comfortable on the love seat. The floor would be a better choice.

"Okay," he said. "You need to freshen up or anything?"

What she needed was a fairy godmother who could either turn her into a woman Eric could love or a robot who wouldn't care one way or the other.

"It will take me just a minute to get ready." She unzipped her suitcase, snatched her makeup kit and fled into the bathroom. One night. That's all she had to survive of this farce of a honeymoon. Then they could both go back to being parents to the twins.

Friends. They wouldn't have to pretend to be anything more.

The realization did nothing to calm her nerves.

WHILE LAURA WAS DOING whatever women did to get ready for dinner, Eric slipped out onto the porch overlooking the ski slopes. He needed some fresh air. Lots of it. The colder the better.

Coming here had been a bad plan.

He'd taken one look at that king-size bed and knew he wanted Laura there with him. Sleep wasn't part of the equation he had in mind.

He'd known for a long time that committing to a woman wasn't in him. He was too damn afraid she'd walk out on him like his mother had. He'd convinced himself no woman would stick with him. So he'd indulged in short-term relationships. When things got too hot, he bailed out.

Mostly, he'd kept himself at arm's length from any woman who even hinted at permanence.

Now he was married. He wanted to make love with Laura.

Unless he screwed up royally, she wasn't likely to leave. Because of the twins. Not because of him.

He wished to God things were different. That he was capable of giving her all she deserved.

He jammed his hands in his pockets and watched the soaring flight of a bald eagle in search of his evening meal, envying the fact that eagles mated for life.

All Eric could do was give Laura the best he had to offer and hope that was enough. His genes didn't come with a how-to book on commitment to a woman. Or vice versa, as nearly as he could tell. No woman had ever committed to him, either.

ONLY A FEW FAMILIES were eating in the high ceilinged dining room, although it was easy to imagine the place packed during the ski season.

Laura nibbled at the chicken salad she'd ordered.

"You don't act like you're very hungry," Eric commented. He'd consumed the better part of a T-bone steak smothered in mushrooms plus a baked potato and green salad.

"I guess I ate too much of Harold's ice cream."

He cocked a skeptical brow. "Really? I didn't see you eat any."

"I'm sorry. Weddings can be pretty nerve-racking."

"Then I've got the perfect antidote. A long soak in the hot tub."

"Eric, I don't think—"

"I won't even peek. I promise."

In truth, the heat of the hot tub might relax her enough so that she could sleep. Even on the floor, if need be.

She pushed her plate away. "I'll take you at your word, Sheriff Oakes."

An obliging grin tilted his lips. "You've got it, Mrs. Oakes."

Her heart pulsed a little harder at his easy use of *Mrs. Oakes*.

Even as they walked back to their room, Laura

wasn't all that sure she could trust Eric's word. Why shouldn't he look? And if he did, would he be disappointed?

She didn't have a great figure. Adequate, she supposed. But hardly model thin. She had no idea what appealed to Eric in a woman physically, or if she had any of the attributes he'd be looking for if their circumstances had been different. On a night like this—in a hot tub—he surely wouldn't be focusing on wit and intelligence.

And she was driving herself crazy over nothing!

She'd get naked, get in the tub and relax. It was no big deal. Eric was in charge of his own thoughts; she wasn't about to change them.

She undressed to her bra and panties in the bathroom, wrapped a big, fluffy towel around her and walked out onto the enclosed porch. Eric was already there, up to his chin in steamy water.

"Remember, no peeking." She slipped off the towel and slid into the water all in one motion. If he'd gotten a glimpse, it was a brief one.

"You cheated," he accused her. "What's with the bra and panties?"

"You *peeked,* so we're even." She shot him an I-knew-you-would grin.

Slowly the heat seeped into her muscles. She leaned back, looking up at the stars sparkling in the black velvet sky. Fancifully, she thought they were winking at her. Wishing her well.

This was the start of her new life. Some things from the past she'd miss—her teaching job, her close relationship with her mother. And she'd continue to grieve the loss of Amy, her little sister.

But she'd managed to keep the twins to raise as her own and find a good man to spend her days with. When one door closed...she thought with a sigh. Today she'd opened a new door.

"This is really nice," she murmured. "Maybe we should put in a hot tub at your place."

"*Our* place, and I'd be willing to consider it." His voice was low and husky, rough with an emotion she couldn't identify.

"Actually, I was kidding."

"I wasn't."

She looked into his pale-blue eyes and found them dark with what could only be sexual desire. Despite the heated water, an even hotter river of response ran through her.

"I know what we said, the rules you wanted," he said. "But I'm only human, Laura. You're a beautiful woman. You have to know what you do to me."

She didn't. Not really. But she did know what he did to her, the thrumming need that had been building in her almost from the first moment they met. If she didn't act now on that need, take advantage of the moment—her honeymoon—when would she?

She stood in the tub. Water sluiced off her body, making her bra and panties transparent, and the cool mountain air struck her, causing her to shiver with both need and desire as she extended her hand. "I'm human, too, Eric."

He was quiet for so long she was afraid she'd made

a dreadful mistake. Read him wrong. As he slowly perused her, she flushed in both mortification and embarrassment, aware her nipples were visible as brown circles beneath her suddenly see-through bra. Instinctively she crossed her arms over herself.

"Don't do that." Standing, he took her hands, gently uncrossing her arms. "I just wanted to look."

His jutting arousal reassured her that he wanted more than a look, and she drew a quick breath. In her imagination she hadn't fully appreciated what a big man he was, hadn't comprehended the strength of his masculinity. Or how feminine he would make her feel.

He slid his hands up her arms, cupping her shoulders in a tender caress. "Are you sure this is what you want?"

She licked her lips and swallowed hard. The heat of the hot tub combined with desire, clashing with the cool air, and she trembled. She was allowing herself the honeymoon she'd always dreamed about. For the moment, she wouldn't allow herself to admit this one night wasn't real. She'd act out the fantasy. Relish the moment. Tomorrow would be time enough to return to reality, to the knowledge that their marriage was based only on their mutual desire to raise the twins.

Her voice shook. "Yes. This is want I want." And more, though she wouldn't allow herself to voice that desire.

Slipping a hand behind her neck, he held her as he

lowered his head to touch her lips in a chaste kiss that held both question and the promise of more to come.

"Yes... Eric... Please."

He didn't ask again as he eased her up out of the hot tub and wrapped her in the thick towel, rubbing away the chill. His kisses followed the path of the towel, first tasting her flesh at the juncture of her throat. Dipping lower to the crest of her breasts, his lips teased near her puckered nipples before he discarded her bra and moved on to her belly.

She groaned at the omission, the ache of wanting to be kissed in exactly the spot he'd missed.

"I'll attend to that detail in a minute or two," he promised, reading her frustration.

She speared her fingers through his neatly trimmed hair and held his head to her as he knelt in front of her, slipping her panties down her legs and worshiping her as she had never before been revered. Her heart soared even as her body pulsed in response to his intimate touch.

The light from inside the room cast a golden reflection across the still water in the hot tub. Steam continued to drift upward. It seemed to catch the scent of the forest, basic and elemental, and bring it back to her. She dragged the fragrance in on quick, excited breaths even as she wanted to fully experience her body joining with Eric's.

"Please...could we..." Go inside, she meant to say but his tongue was doing wonderful, impossible things to her and she couldn't think...couldn't speak coherently.

Her explosive release caught her off guard, so sudden and powerful. She cried out. Her legs wobbled, weak as rubber.

He stood, drawing his work-roughened palms up over her hips and midriff until his thumbs slicked over her nipples. His intense, glittering gaze locked on hers and he smiled triumphantly. He pulled her close, letting her feel his arousal pressed against her belly.

"I think it's time to go inside now," he said.

Steadying herself with her hands on his chest, she nodded. "Good plan."

To her surprise, he scooped her into his arms, carrying her over the threshold into their room. She'd never felt so cherished, so at the mercy of her own desire and that of a man. If this was the only night she'd experience this total immersion in Eric's searing sensuality, then so be it. She'd have this memory to last her a lifetime. Tomorrow would be time enough for the marriage of convenience she'd been so determined to insist upon.

The mattress was firm, the sheet cool on her back as he laid her down. He stretched out beside her and looked into her eyes, smiling slightly.

"Rory was right," he said, his voice husky.

She arched her brows.

"Honeymoons are worth doing."

He captured her mouth in the kind of kiss she'd longed to share with Eric. Hot, moist and deep. His avid exploration with his tongue stole her breath. She responded with matching abandon.

She clutched his shoulders as his hand kneaded her

breast. Her nipple hardened and beaded beneath his palm. Between her thighs where she was still sensitive from her earlier climax, moisture flowed again at his slightest touch.

She moaned. "I want you."

"There's one more thing I want to do first. I promised."

His mouth covered her breast. He laved and suckled, driving her wild. She sobbed, trying to get closer to him, struggling to become one with him. To her amazement, another climax burst through her.

"Oh, my!" she gasped. "I never thought I'd—"

"You're going to do it again, too."

She didn't have time to think, to recover, before he spread her legs. He took his time easing into her, moving with an erotic slowness that aroused her again simply because of his caution. His caring ways brought tears of gratitude to her eyes.

"Wrap your legs around me, Blue Eyes."

Smiling at the nickname he'd given her, she did as he asked, and he thrust into her, stretching her. She clenched around the hard, pulsing length of him, accepting him, and she wanted to cry out in celebration that they were a perfect match. She rode a glorious edge between victory and surrender as he pumped into her. Muffling her cries against his throat, she tasted the salty flavor of his skin, inhaled his scent, as rich and elemental as the forest outside their door.

Her heart took one final leap to a place from which there was no return. Light splintered into a million shards and she was lost in another world.

Eric gathered her into his arms as his body jerked with his final release, pulsing deeply within her. Had he ever known a more responsive woman? One who gave so much of herself? Not in this lifetime.

Her taste was still in his mouth, on his lips, as he rolled to his side, bringing her with him. He kissed the damp hair at her temple as she curled against him. Kissed her lips. Felt his body go weak.

With what little energy he still retained, he asked, "You okay?"

Her cheek moved against his chest, and he sensed she was smiling. "What happened to the handcuffs?"

"Darn. Must have left 'em in the truck."

She cuddled closer.

That was the last awareness he had before dawn eased its way through the open window.

Disoriented by the unfamiliar surroundings, he rolled over. Immediately the memory of the night returned to him along with a sense of regret that the other side of the bed was empty. Only Laura's feminine scent remained on the pillow, and the sight of rumpled sheets gave evidence of the night they'd shared.

He spotted her standing on the deck outside watching the morning light turn the sky from pale rose to a crystalline blue. Her nightgown and sheer robe allowed him to see only the shadow of her silhouette. That was enough to cause a low, harsh groan to escape as he realized how much he wanted her back in bed again.

So much for their in-name-only agreement.

Unless Laura regretted last night.

Swinging his legs over the side of the bed, he found his shorts and tugged them on. He pulled the sliding door open but she didn't turn around.

"What's up, Blue Eyes?"

"I was just thinking how nice it would be to stay here longer."

"Uh, we could do that." He'd be happy to play hot tub tag all day long, if she was willing.

Turning, she smiled, and he didn't see any regret in her eyes, but there were questions.

"That wouldn't be fair to Kristi and Rory. They only volunteered to baby-sit the twins for one night."

"I could call. See if they could manage another day or two."

She rubbed her bare arms against the cool of the morning air, her skin as soft as silk, he remembered, and she seemed to consider the possibility.

Slowly she shook her head. "No, I think we'd better go home."

"If that's what you'd like." He didn't want to press the issue. It was her decision to make. She'd set the ground rules initially.

After last night he had a pretty good idea those rules could be modified.

If he played his cards right.

"Eric?" She turned away as though she couldn't quite bring herself to face him. "When we get home—"

"Yeah?" He cringed at the question he knew she was asking. Not about having more sex. He could handle that, big-time. But about what their relationship would be. A question about love.

"After last night, I was wondering—"

"Laura, honey, you gotta remember who I am. Last night was terrific—more than terrific." He stepped forward, touched his hand to her shoulder but she moved away, no doubt guessing what he was about to say. "But I'm not sure I know how to love a woman. I've given my vow I'll be faithful to you, and that won't be a problem. But I'm not sure I can ever give you anything more than that." He dropped his hand to his side. "I'm sorry."

Her head lowered, as though she had suddenly discovered some new fascination with her toes. "Why don't we pack up and get home. The twins probably miss us."

Eric cursed himself for being less than the man he should be. But hey, life sucked sometimes. He'd do the very best he could for Laura...and the twins.

That, at least, was something she could take to the bank.

THEY RETURNED HOME by early afternoon, and Laura carried her suitcase upstairs to her room, dropping it on her bed. There was so much she had to do—arrange to have her furniture and personal possessions packed and shipped to Grass Valley, sell her condo, change her name on her driver's license and social security, myriad tasks that would take weeks to accomplish.

She turned, surprised to find Eric had followed her and was leaning against the doorjamb.

"I thought I'd clean the stuff out of my closet, make room for your things."

She hesitated for a moment. If only he'd spoken words of love to her last night, she would leap at the chance to move in with him. But that hadn't happen. To the contrary, he'd denied any feelings for her.

"I thought we'd go back to the way we were." The absence of those all-important words, his love, created a dissonant chord in her conscience.

He lifted his shoulders in a lazy shrug. "Seems to me that we've already let the horse out of the barn, as it were. And we do have to keep up our image that we're married. For the sake of the twins."

When she didn't immediately respond, he said, "If it'll help, I'll let you use the handcuffs next time."

She stifled a laugh as the thought of him bound to the headboard became an intriguingly vivid picture in her mind. It wasn't an offer of commitment by a long shot but it was intriguing. "If you're sure."

"About the handcuffs? We'll see about that. But you sharing my room and my bed? Yeah, I'm sure." He nodded. "Let's go get the twins, and I'll start cleaning out my closet."

She didn't know how to react to her changing circumstances. She'd never believed in sex simply for the sake of sex. Her emotions had to be involved. With Eric, they certainly were.

Did sleeping with him mean she'd compromised her principles?

Yet if he still wanted her, how could she say no now that she had once experienced the passion he offered?

"ISN'T THAT HOT TUB the greatest?" Kristi asked.

The twins were sleeping, and she'd trapped Laura in the kitchen while the men were outside discussing important things, like which football team would make it to the Super Bowl this year. Out the window, Laura could see Adam circling the driveway on his bike, Ruff close on the boy's heels.

She felt her cheeks warm at the memory of her honeymoon. "Yes, the hot tub was very nice. Eric's thinking about putting in one at the house."

"Oh, a man after my own heart. I'll have to mention that to Rory." She rinsed the last of what appeared to be lunch dishes and set them on the rack to dry. "So tell me everything that happened. How did it go with you two?"

"You want every intimate detail? Or just the highlights?"

"Well, I am a trained medical professional," she said with mock seriousness, her eyes sparkling. "You're welcome to tell me anything you'd like, confident my lips are forever sealed."

Laura laughed. "I'd rather hear how you got along with the twins."

"They were wonderful." Sighing, she looked dreamy. "I can hardly wait to have another baby. Rory, on the other hand, was something less than enthusiastic at three in the morning."

"I know the feeling." Although, that quiet hour in the dark of night was precious to Laura, most especially when she shared those moments with Eric.

She heard a baby waking in the other room. Love welled up in her chest and she hurried toward the cry. "Mommy's coming, honey."

Whatever else might happen in the weeks and years ahead, she would always be Becky's and Mandy's mother. By marrying Eric, she had solidified her position. And she loved him for it.

Chapter Eleven

"Maybe that chair would look better next to the window."

Eric leaned on the wing chair that the movers had brought from Laura's condo, exhaling a weary breath. "That's where it was a half hour ago. *Before* you had me put it next to the fireplace, which was after you wanted it over by the stairs."

Laura winced. "I know. It's just so hard to mix and match our furniture together." His was dark wood and leather, hers was blond wood and pastels. They might not clash, exactly, but they didn't blend, either.

"I've got a really great idea." He plopped down in the chair, extending his legs. A sheen of sweat dampened his forehead. "Why don't I call a thrift shop in Great Falls, have them pick up the whole kit and caboodle, and we'll start over from scratch."

"No," she gasped. Her hand trembled as she shoved back her hair from her face. "All this furniture is perfectly fine. I just need to figure out—"

He propelled himself out of the chair, and the next

thing she knew his arms were wrapped around her. They'd been married ten whole days—and nights. From their wedding night, he'd maintained he wasn't capable of love. Despite that, she wouldn't have given up a moment of the nights she'd spent in his arms.

She'd learned Eric's body as intimately as a woman could—the feel of his flat belly beneath her palm, the ripple of muscles across his shoulders as he entered her, the light furring of hair on his legs and the dreadful scar left by his rodeo accident.

In return, he'd learned every inch of her body, kissed every centimeter and found erogenous zones she hadn't known existed.

Despite all of that, she would have happily sacrificed dealing with the mess the arrival of her things from Helena had caused. Even though she had given her dining room set to a neighbor, plus a few odds and ends, there were boxes stacked everywhere. The thought of unpacking it all while trying to care for the twins was nearly overwhelming. She still had to list her condo with a real estate agent, arrange to have the carpets cleaned. The tasks seemed endless.

In spite of all the pressure, perhaps her tension was in large measure due to her own ambivalent feelings. Only time would tell if she'd done the right thing by choosing to marry Eric without his love.

"If I'd realized how hard this would be, I could have given the rest of my things to charity in Helena and saved the price of moving it here." She rested her head on his shoulder. He was so sturdy, such a rock. At least, he had been through the first three hours of rearranging furniture after the movers had left. Now he appeared to be faltering. Who could blame him?

"We'll work it out. You could use a sitting room upstairs. You know, somewhere to get away from the twins."

She eyed him skeptically. "Which of these pieces of furniture would you like to carry upstairs?"

He groaned. "Good point. Maybe I'd better put in an emergency call to my brothers, round up some strong backs."

Her laugh was cut off by the doorbell ringing. Almost no one in Grass Valley did anything but knock. And then they were as likely as not to go to the back door and let themselves in.

Eric planted a quick kiss on her lips. "I'll see who that is. With any luck it will be some weight lifter who's looking for a good workout."

While he went to answer the door, Laura scanned the room. There had to be some way for all of this mismatched furniture to work together. A blending of tastes. But for the life of her, she couldn't see how. Clearly she'd spent too much time reading about history and not enough learning the ins and outs of home decoration.

Perhaps Eric's idea of an upstairs sitting room would be the best use of the furniture.

As she considered the possibility, Laura became aware Eric hadn't returned from answering the door, and she could now hear masculine voices. Voices that were less than friendly.

She stepped to the door, opening it to find Eric talking to a tall man with stringy blond hair and tattoos on his forearms. Eric's wide-legged stance was aggressive; the stranger appeared to be mocking him.

"Eric?"

He turned, his expression strained. "This is Russ Ungar. He claims he's the father of the twins."

For a moment Eric's words didn't register. Then all of the blood drained from Laura's head, and she thought she was going to faint. Her stomach knotted on a wave of nausea. This wasn't happening. It couldn't. A biological father had rights that no one could counter—not a foster sibling, as she had been to Amy. Or a half brother, as Eric was to Amy. The fact that they both loved the twins beyond reason wouldn't matter in the face of his paternal rights.

But he was an abuser. Amy had worn the bruises he'd inflicted the day she moved into Laura's condo. The man didn't deserve to walk the face of the earth, much less be a father to his children. Assuming he *was* their father.

"How do we know you're who you say you are?" she asked.

"I've been asking the same question," Eric said.

"For now, you'll just have to trust me, sweet cheeks." He glanced around the porch and to the outbuildings. "Looks like you landed yourself some nice digs."

She straightened her spine, prepared to block him from the house and access to the twins, if need be. "What do you want?"

He leaned back against the porch railing as though he were a neighbor dropping by for a friendly visit. "I went looking for Amy at your condo, honey bunch," he said to Laura. "She talked a lot about you. Loving sister and all that."

"You're a little late to express your condolences, if that's what you're after."

Ignoring her comment, he said, "The neighbors told me what happened. That's real sad, her passing and all." He didn't look at all remorseful. *Bored* was closer to the truth.

"How about getting to the point, Mr. Ungar," Eric said. "My wife asked you what you wanted."

"The neighbors also told me you and this cowboy got married—and kidnapped my sweet little babies."

Laura gasped. "We did no such thing!"

"It's time for you leave, Mr. Ungar." Eric stepped between Laura and the stranger, giving him little room to maneuver. "You're trespassing on private property."

Alarmed, Laura realized Russ Ungar was an inch or two taller than Eric and lean as a whip. She knew Eric was strong and quick, but doubted the man cared about fighting fair, which gave Russ Ungar the advantage over an honest man. And Eric's gun was locked away in the safe in the kitchen where he always kept it when he was at home, for safety's sake.

Laura wished he had it strapped to his hip.

"Don't get your shorts in a knot, cowboy."

"*Sheriff* Oakes to you, Mr. Ungar. Now, let's move it off the porch."

The man didn't budge. "Well now, since you're the law around here, you must know all about parental rights. Seems to me I've got plenty. Don't you agree?"

"You're not going to take the twins," Laura stated

emphatically. She'd give her own life first before allowing the man who had abused Amy to have them.

Eric stood his ground, as determined as Laura. "You'll have to prove whatever rights you've got in a court of law. I suggest you get yourself a very good attorney because we'll fight you every inch of the way. From what Laura has told me, assuming you are who you say you are, you'd have a lot to answer for in front of a judge."

His lips twitched into a smirk again. "You're scaring me, Sheriff," he said sarcastically. "Amy's dead. All you've got is hearsay, and that's not gonna cut it in a courtroom."

"I find it interesting you didn't deny my accusation. The sign of a guilty man, I'd say."

Eric gestured toward the man's car just as Laura heard Becky's wake-up cry over the baby monitor in the living room.

Ungar shot a glance in that direction, then raised his eyes toward the second floor. "Ain't that the purdiest sound you ever heard? I think I'll go on upstairs and say howdy to my little darlings."

"No!" Laura cried.

He managed one step toward the door before Eric had him in an arm lock.

Ungar struggled against Eric's forceful grip. "Hey! You're hurting me, dammit! I'll have you charged with assault."

"Walk, Ungar, or I'll break your damn arm."

Continuing to manhandle him, Eric marched him to his car, which was parked out front. He slammed Ungar against the side of the vehicle. Holding him there, he used his free hand to open the driver's door.

"You got any weapons in there, Ungar?"

"None of your damn business."

Cursing himself because his own weapon was safely locked away, Eric called to Laura. "Get back inside and lock the doors. Call Rory and tell him what's going on. Tell him I need backup. Then stay with the twins."

He glanced around under the driver's seat as best he could. Except for an empty cigarette pack, it looked clean. But that didn't mean the guy didn't have a weapon stashed in the glove box or trunk. He wasn't going to take the risk that Ungar could get to his gun before Eric could get to his revolver inside the house.

He'd wait for backup.

"Let me go, man," Ungar complained. "You're busting my shoulder."

"Gee, I feel real sorry about that." He yanked Ungar's arm a little higher.

"You can't keep me away from my own kids if I want to see them."

"You aren't going anywhere near the twins without proof of who you are and a court order." Which he just might be able to get, damn it to hell. *If* he was their father.

A minute later, Rory trotted up, shotgun cradled in his arm. "Whatcha got?"

"A sleazebag." Eric wrestled Ungar to the front of the car. "Nice and easy now. I'm going to let you go and I want you spread-eagled on the hood. You know the drill." From the looks of Ungar's tattoos, which were pretty rough, they'd been done by a prison artist. All the more reason to keep him away from the twins.

Once Ungar was in position, his feet and arms spread wide, Rory pressed the shotgun to the small of his back. "Keep in mind I've got a real itchy finger when it comes to guys who abuse women," he said.

Eric didn't doubt his brother would pull the trigger if he had to. His sympathy toward dumb animals didn't stretch to punks like Ungar.

A quick search of the car didn't turn up any guns. Eric wished it had. He'd bet his badge the guy was on parole. A weapons violation would send him back to prison. Which would be fine with Eric.

He backed away from the car. "He's clean," he told Rory.

His brother lifted his shotgun. "No quick moves. I'm still feeling real twitchy."

Straightening, Ungar gave Eric a malevolent glare. "Don't get cocky, Sheriff. I'll be back."

"You'd be smarter not to bother."

He sneered and got into his car. The engine cranked over. He shifted into reverse, hit the gas and kicked up gravel as he backed away.

Eric and Rory watched as the car peeled out onto the main street.

"I didn't like the sound of any of that." Rory popped the shells from the shotgun. "Laura says he's the twins' father?"

"That's what he claims." The adrenaline that had flooded his system slowly ebbed away, leaving Eric more worried about the threat Ungar presented than he'd care to admit. "Thanks for backing me up."

"No problem."

"I've gotta check on Laura and the twins." He also intended to give Laura the combination to his gun safe and teach her how to use a weapon. He didn't want to leave his wife unprotected. Or the twins.

And as soon as he was sure Laura was okay, he was going to do a computer check on that Ungar character. He was hoping there was a warrant out on the guy. That would take care of the problem. Temporarily.

Inside, he took the stairs two at a time. The door to the nursery was closed.

He rapped his knuckles lightly on the door. "Laura, it's me." He eased the door open.

Her eyes were wide, her fair complexion pale as she looked up at him. While she was feeding a bottle to Becky, the most telling thing was the carving knife on the table beside the rocking chair.

"He's gone," Eric said.

"He'll be back, won't he?"

"Probably."

Silent tears flooded her eyes and spilled down her cheeks. "Why would a man like that want our babies?"

Our babies. His throat tightened on the impact of her words.

"I don't know." In fact, it seemed odd. It would be more reasonable for him to be grateful not to be stuck with child-support payments—assuming he even had a job.

"I won't let him take my babies." She swallowed a sob and tilted her chin at a stubborn angle. "If I have to, I'll take them away. Start a new life in a place where no one will find me."

Her words cut through his gut as painfully as though she'd used the carving knife on him. She hadn't meant the twins were as much his as hers. She would leave him in a heartbeat—for the sake of the twins.

He knelt beside her, stroking Becky's head. "He won't get the twins. I swear it on my word of honor."

She touched him then, the trembling brush of her fingertips across his hair. "Thank you."

He chided himself for wanting more than her gratitude.

Fear twisted through his gut. What if he couldn't keep his vow? What if they did lose the twins to Russ Ungar? Would Laura want to stay with him?

"Can you find out something about that man? Maybe you can arrest him for something if he comes back."

"I plan to do exactly that—check wants and warrants—as soon as I can get to the computer in my office. He's sure to be in the system somewhere. I'd bet my Stetson he picked up those tattoos in prison."

"He's an ex-convict?"

"That would be my surmise."

She grabbed her lip between her teeth, and her chin trembled. "Do you think he really was Amy's boyfriend? Why would she pick a man like—"

"I don't know." He couldn't imagine any woman wanting to be with Russ Ungar, but he'd seen women make some dumb choices—and pay for it with broken bones and sometimes their lives. "I'm going to try to find out."

Taking her hand, he pressed a kiss to her palm. Laura and the twins were his family now. He wasn't going to let anything happen to them.

To his dismay, a few minutes later at his office, he

discovered the state computer system was down—again. His background search on Ungar would have to wait until the morning.

AFTER THE TWINS had their nighttime bottles, Eric went to take a shower. Laura promised she'd be along in a minute. But when he returned to the bedroom, she wasn't there.

Troubled, he walked down the hall to the nursery. He found Laura rocking Mandy, who was asleep. Becky was in the crib right next to them, her eyes closed, her little arms and legs as relaxed as only a baby could be.

Their mother appeared considerably more tense.

"I thought you were coming to bed when the twins were settled," he whispered. Holding Laura at night, loving her, he was able to think of Laura as his. Not his wife because of her love for the twins. But *his*—her soft skin that smelled of baby powder, her hair that carried the scent of lemon shampoo, the open response she gave him. All his to explore, to possess. Not an illusion that could easily vanish under the harsh light of day or the threat of a paternity claim.

"I can't seem to leave them." Her chair moved back and forth in a hypnotizing rhythm. "I keep thinking that man will show up and snatch them away from us."

"He's not coming back tonight. I promise." Gently he lifted Mandy from her arms and placed the baby in the second crib, the one the movers had brought from Laura's condo this morning. Little Bo Peep and her sheep were scattered across the sheet and bumper pads.

"I don't think I'll be able to sleep," Laura protested when he took her hand.

"Then just let me hold you." He needed the reassurance as much as she did. Sleep wouldn't come easily to either of them tonight.

Laura allowed him to guide her to their bedroom. If anyone could drive her fears away, lift the encroaching shadows that plagued her, it would be Eric. She trusted him in ways she'd never trusted another man. Her heart demanded that of her even while her intellect warned her to be cautious, that she was risking heartbreak.

She ignored the niggling voice of reason. For better or worse, she'd married Eric Oakes. She intended to stay that way unless and until he made it clear he no longer wanted her.

A shudder of apprehension went through her as she realized that might happen if their chance to raise the twins together evaporated because of Russ Ungar.

These were the only children she'd ever be able to offer him.

"Don't think about it," Eric urged. He tugged her knit top off over her head. "He's not going to bother us tonight."

"I know. It's silly of me." She toed off her shoes, all too aware that Eric was wearing only his briefs, his arousal evident. His physical presence had become familiar to her. The breadth of his chest, his muscular legs and the jagged scar on his thigh from surgery following his rodeo injury. Everything about him was so beautifully masculine, she could imagine him as a Greek god come alive from the pages of one of her history books. Surely he had the power to protect her…and the twins.

"Nothing you do is silly."

Her gaze dropped below his waist. Despite his appeal, her own pang of loneliness and need, she turned away from him. "I'm sorry. I don't think I can do it tonight. I'm so stressed—"

"We're just going to hold each other, Laura. That's all. Because my body responds to you doesn't mean I have to act on it."

Reaching for her nightgown, she slipped it on. "It doesn't seem fair to you."

"I promise I'll survive." He pulled back the covers for her.

Gratefully she eased down onto the bed, snuggling as he tucked her in. The ache of fatigue and tension tugged at her, and she curled onto her side.

The light clicked off. Behind her the mattress dipped as he crawled into bed, too. He wrapped his arm around her, spooning her against the warmth of his body. The weight of his arm, locked around her midsection, protected her. His breath across her cheek was a gentle caress. This is what she needed. To be guarded, her fears eased while she slept.

Except, the press of his arousal against her buttocks awakened another need she had—not to be protected but to be loved. Desire stirred within her.

The sensation, the urge, rose slowly, and she turned in his arms, placing a kiss on his lips. "Does a woman have a right to change her mind?"

"I'd say that right is probably in the constitution someplace. And I'm sworn to uphold the laws of the state and the constitution."

"I'm glad."

She claimed his mouth and that was all the encouragement he needed. His loving was gentle, as familiar as breathing, as hopeful as the sun after a stormy day.

Except for their rasping breaths, the house was silent. The stillness blanketed them like a velvet shield. No one could enter, no one could bring them harm.

Their hands caressed, soothed and explored. Aroused. Their lips and tongues did the same across plains and valleys that they had each intimately learned about the other.

When he slipped into her, she arched up in welcome. In return, he drove away the darkness that had entered her soul. Together they soared into a light that was brighter than dawn and more enduring, if only they could cling to each other.

AT BREAKFAST THE NEXT MORNING, Eric sipped his coffee thoughtfully. He'd dressed for work. In contrast, Laura was wearing a cozy flannel robe against the cool fall-like air. She'd brushed her hair into place but hadn't yet applied her makeup. He liked her that way, her cheeks a natural rosy color, her complexion as fair as sweet cream. Heck, he liked seeing her across the table from him morning, noon and night, dressed any way she chose.

He cleared his throat. "How'd you sleep last night?"

"Better than I thought I would." She smiled wryly. "You're a good antidote for my stress."

"Glad I could oblige."

Unfortunately, he hadn't slept as well. His brain

had kept turning over ideas, searching for ways to block Russ Ungar's next move, if he intended to make one.

"I've got to get to the office, see if the state computer system is back in service."

"I'm not sure what I hope you'll find." She spread butter on her toast and took a dainty bite. "If he has a criminal record, which you think he does, that could make him all the more dangerous. But if he's wanted for something now, you could send him to prison for the next hundred years or so. That would keep him occupied long enough for the twins to grow up."

"Frankly I'm hoping to discover he couldn't possibly be the twins' father. That would solve the problem."

Thoughtful creases bisected her forehead. "You mean, if he had been in prison at the time Amy got pregnant?"

"Something like that. Assuming no conjugal visits, of course."

"That would be perfect. Even if Ungar decided not to exert his so-called paternity rights, I'd hate to have to tell the twins someday that the man we met yesterday was their biological father." She visibly shuddered. "I'd rather not have them know."

"I'm not so sure about that." Shoving back his chair, he stood and carried his mug to the coffeepot for a refill. "My father is named on my birth certificate, but I don't have any memory of him. I always wondered if I was like him. Or if I'd want to be."

"Pray the girls never want to be like Russ Ungar."

"Yeah, I know. You sure Amy never said anything about her boyfriend? Let his name slip, even once?

Or mentioned what he looked like or did for a living? Any hint?''

"Not that I can recall. I think she was embarrassed she'd gone off with him and then stayed as long as she did. It wasn't until she knew she was pregnant and decided not to put her baby at risk that she finally ran away."

"Abusers have a knack for convincing a woman he's going to reform. Or that getting knocked around is somehow her fault." He leaned back against the counter, his fingers wrapped around the mug. "Whatever happens, someday the twins will want to know about their father. What kind of a man he was."

"They'll have you as a role model." A smile softened her worry lines. "You'll be the one to teach them what a good man is like."

"You think?"

She nodded. "I know. Assuming we can ward off the threat Ungar represents. You promised we could."

He downed another slug of coffee and set the mug on the counter. "Guess I'd better get busy, then. I'll give Rory a call, see if he can come over to stay with you."

"Why?" She looked surprised by his suggestion.

"I don't like the idea of you and the twins being alone. Ungar's a wild card—"

"I'll be fine, Eric. Your office is less than the length of a football field away. For that matter, if he shows up while you're there, you'd see his car going by."

He weighed his concern for Laura's safety against the risk of leaving her alone. "All right," he said cautiously. "But I want you to lock the doors after I'm gone and stay inside."

Never in the time he'd lived in Grass Valley had he locked his doors. It hadn't been necessary.

For the safety of Laura and the twins, today it was.

Chapter Twelve

Picnic tables with colorful paper tablecloths and plates were set up near the ranch house at the Double O to celebrate little Nancy's third birthday. Balloons tied to the tables tugged at their strings in a light breeze. Her first-ever birthday cake had Nancy dancing around, as excited as a butterfly just emerged from its cocoon.

For Laura the party provided a respite from worries about Russ Ungar. They hadn't heard a word directly from him in three days, although Eric was still checking his sources to get more information about the man beyond his prison record.

She fervently hoped Ungar had decided not to make trouble over the twins.

Once the cake and ice cream had been demolished, the teenage cadre of Oakes boys rounded up the younger guests to give them horseback rides in the corral.

Laura smiled at the thought of the twins' first birthday and what she would do to celebrate that milestone event. She glanced at the babies napping in their playpen in a shady spot on the porch. Please, God, let them still be hers to raise when they turned one year old. And twenty-one, for that matter, although they might not appreciate motherly interference at that age.

Kristi, looking a little haggard, joined her at the edge of the porch. "I don't know how Lizzie does it. A gazillion kids of all ages, noisy as all get-out, screaming and shouting, and she looks as cool as though she'd just stepped off the pages of *Glamour*."

Laughing, Laura said, "I suspect she's pleased we didn't get an afternoon thundershower to drive the party indoors. That might have been a bit much even for her."

"I don't know. She's one of those people you want to have around in a disaster. Never seems to lose her head. My guess is that she had a contingency plan all worked out."

She boosted herself up onto the porch railing, a woman comfortable in her own skin. Although both of Laura's sisters-in-law were a few years younger than she was, they appeared to have their acts very much together. They were also smart and fun to be around. Laura didn't feel nearly as confident of herself since her marriage as she had before. Then, although she'd often been lonely and heartsick at the knowledge she'd never have children of her own, she'd worked her way into a comfortable niche teaching history to adolescents. Cramming it down their respective craws, if need be.

Now the rules had changed. Her whole *life* had changed, and sometimes she felt as though she was walking a tightrope. Maybe if Eric loved her, she wouldn't feel like an imposter, that she belonged here as a member of the Oakes family. But Eric didn't believe he was capable of the love she so desperately wanted, which made her feel vulnerable. Someday he might meet a woman he *could* love, and she would have to give him up.

"Have you heard anything more from that guy Rory helped Eric run off?" Kristi asked.

Mentally, Laura shook away her troubling thoughts. "Not a word, thank goodness. Eric checked him out. Russ Ungar not only has a record for petty crimes, he spent almost a year in the Montana State Prison in Deer Lodge."

"Well then, he couldn't be the twins' father, right?"

"Unfortunately, he'd been arrested but was out on bail about the time my foster sister, the twins' mother, must have gotten pregnant."

"So this Ungar character could be the girls' biological father?"

"Just because he wasn't in jail doesn't prove anything about paternity." She'd been telling herself that for the past two days, since Eric did the data search. Somehow it wasn't all that reassuring.

Carrying baby Susie on her hip, Lizzie strolled over to them, her blond hair still neatly held in place by a gold clip at the back of her neck. She lowered Susie to the ground, and the toddler took off for the porch steps to visit the twins.

"Don't wake the babies," Lizzie admonished.

She gave Kristi and Laura a weary smile. "I swear, I've managed parties for three hundred guests at the fanciest country club in Marin County that weren't as exhausting as this."

Kristi clapped her hands. "Heaven be praised! She's human."

Lizzie looked at Laura, puzzled.

"I think she's pleased you're as exhausted as she is," Laura explained, "what with all the commotion. It's been a wonderful party. All the children have enjoyed themselves."

"Thank you. But the truth is, I do have another reason to feel so tired."

"Oh?" Laura and Kristi said in unison.

Lizzie's smile was just this side of smug. "I'm pregnant."

"Oh my God!" Kristi wailed. "That's wonderful!"

"Congratulations. I'm happy for you," Laura said. She was pleased, even though the familiar pang of regret that she'd never have her own child caught her off guard for a moment. She had the twins. An enormous blessing she'd never anticipated. "Walker, in particular, must be thrilled."

"We both are." Lizzie grinned. "Although I don't think either of us had ever imagined we'd have *seven* children."

"Mercy, no," Laura said with a laugh. She'd be content with two.

Kristi hopped down from her perch. "Guess what?

I'm pregnant, too. We'll be able to raise our babies together.''

Lizzie opened her mouth and let out an unladylike scream. "That's wonderful!" She wrapped her arms around Kristi, and the two women hugged each other, laughing and crying at the same time.

Susie toddled to the porch railing, extending her arms. "Mamamama," she babbled.

Pressing her lips together, Laura couldn't recall a time when she'd felt so left out. It wasn't the fault of these two women who had so recently become her friends. She'd simply never be able to join the sorority of women who had given birth to a child.

If Russ Ungar had his way, she might not be able to lay claim to her one chance at motherhood.

KRISTI AND LIZZIE were each feeding a twin in the ranch house living room when Eric strolled inside.

He tipped his Stetson to the back of his head. "Now that's quite a sight."

"Your sisters-in-law are getting in practice for their own little bundles of joy," Laura said. "They're both expecting."

"Really?" He grinned. "Son of a gun. Sounds like my brothers have been busy."

"If you're like the rest of the Oakes boys," Kristi said, "I'll wager Laura will be joining us in maternity clothes not too long from now."

Eric snapped his head toward Laura, and she looked away, making a concerted effort not to let the pain show on her face.

"Sorry, ladies, I'm afraid that's not possible." Picking up a receiving blanket, she folded it carefully in her lap. "I'm not physically able to have a baby."

Kristi gasped, and Lizzie eyes widened in surprise.

"There's a lot being done in the fertility arena these days," Kristi said. "It's possible that whatever the problem is, there could be a way—"

"Not in my case. My uterus was removed when I was sixteen." Uncomfortable with the conversation, Laura stood, though she didn't quite know where to go or how to hide from her greatest flaw.

Eric rescued her by taking her hand and tugging her close to him. "I had this great idea, which is why I came looking for you. Since we've got a whole cadre of baby-sitters available, how 'bout I take you riding? I'll give you a minitour of the ranch."

However grateful Laura was for the change of subject, she didn't think it was right for her to take advantage of the two women who'd been so kind to her since she arrived in Grass Valley. "They've both been working hard all day. It wouldn't be fair to dump the twins on—"

"Don't be silly." Lifting Becky to her shoulder, Lizzie patted the baby's back. "The twins aren't any trouble, Susie will be down with her nap for another hour or two, and you don't get many chances to get away from the babies. Besides, Walker has everything under control outside. Go on while you can."

Laura glanced at Kristi.

"We'll be fine here." Her smile held a wealth of both understanding and sympathy, an ability which no doubt served her well in her role as a nurse. "Enjoy yourself."

Not allowing Laura to object further, Eric led her out of the house through the back door, grabbing a spare hat for her from the mud room as they went.

"We'll commandeer one of the mares for you that the kids have been riding, and I'll saddle up a gelding."

"You sure you won't get an argument from Nancy or one of her friends?" she asked.

"Last time I looked, the three-year-old set was feeding carrots to a couple of rabbits Walker got her for her birthday."

"I hope he has them in separate cages or he'll have more bunnies than he counted on."

The family's black-and-white Border collie followed them into the barn, where Eric hefted a saddle from a rack in the tack room, carrying it to the stall of an Appaloosa. The air was cool and rich with the aroma of hay and horses. Dust motes twisted in a column of sunlight that slanted through the open doorway.

"Sorry Kristi and Lizzie made you feel uncomfortable back there," he said.

"They're not the problem." She was, or rather her reproductive system was. "It's just as well they know the truth so they won't start wondering what's wrong with you when I don't get pregnant."

"Nothing's wrong with either of us." Canting his head, he slipped beneath the brim of her hat to give her a quick kiss.

A shimmer of pleasure slid through Laura's midsection. She marveled that a simple kiss could erase the bitter sense of failure that plagued her whenever she thought about being barren. His touch was like a healing balm on her soul.

With practiced hands, he saddled the gelding. Every movement had its own beauty, a masculine dance that was both graceful and a communion between the man and the animal.

He led the horse outside and looped the reins over the corral fence next to the mare he'd chosen for Laura to ride.

He glanced down at her casual running shoes. "Looks like we're going to have to get you some riding boots."

"These will be fine as long as you don't expect me to leap six-foot fences."

"This is cow country, Blue Eyes. The sheriff's best girl ought to have proper riding equipment."

"The next time we go to Great Falls," she promised with a smile. In her old life, she'd never imagined needing riding boots except for doing a Texas two-step on a Saturday night. In Grass Valley, they were de rigueur every day of the week.

He cupped his hands near the stirrup. "Up you go."

Mounting, she drew a quick breath. "Oh my, I don't think I've been on a horse since high school. I'd forgotten how high you are up here."

"You okay?"

If Eric could find it in his heart to love her, she'd

be terrific. "I'm fine. Fortunately, altitude doesn't give me a nosebleed."

He chuckled as he adjusted her stirrups, from time to time grasping her calves or running his palm along her thigh with casual intimacy. Whether she was fully dressed or stark naked, his lightest caress aroused a deep passion within her. Since their wedding night, she'd developed a serious addiction to making love with Eric. Never with any other man had she been so sexually ravenous.

With a sigh, she realized she might never get enough of the man to satisfy her cravings.

He gave one last tug to the stirrup. "Something wrong?"

"Not at the moment."

He mounted his gelding, and they rode away from the corral, the Border collie trotting along behind them.

"Is it all right that the dog's coming, too?" she asked.

"Bandit likes to hunt rabbits and prairie dogs when he gets a chance."

"I hope he doesn't catch one while I'm around." She had a soft heart for little creatures.

"I don't think we have to worry about that. He's not as fast as he used to be."

"For which I'll count my blessings."

After the heat of summer, the prairie grass had turned golden brown, and stretched out across the land like ocean waves shifting in the light breeze. Bandit's zigzag course roused a quail into flight. With a bark, he leaped into the air, jaws snapping, but the bird was long gone.

"That dog must have tried to catch a thousand quail over the years and hasn't caught one yet," Eric commented. "You'd think he'd learn."

"He probably thinks it's a game and he's winning."

"Yeah. You ever have a dog when you were a kid?"

"We had a wirehaired terrier when I was about five. His name was Spiffy and he loved to lick my ice-cream cone, which mother abhorred, of course."

"Understandably. Germs and all." He quirked a grin.

"Mmm. Unfortunately, he also liked to hop over our backyard fence and dig up the neighbor's flower beds."

"I bet that made him popular around the neighborhood."

"We added about three more feet to the fence, but Spiffy still made it over the top. Or dug underneath it. Finally Dad gave the dog to a friend who had some acreage outside of town and a fenced doggy run. But my ice cream never tasted quite the same after that."

"Maybe we can talk to Harold at the pharmacy about a new flavor of the month."

"Why don't we keep that idea to ourselves for now?" She shuddered daintily. "Mother got a poodle a couple of years ago for company."

"Out here a poodle wouldn't last long. Too many predators."

Laura adjusted easily to the motion of the horse, and they rode along in comfortable silence. Once Bandit spotted something in the grass and raced off out of sight only to trot back minutes later, rejoining them with no sign that he'd caught anything.

In the distance the mountains were purple shadowed as the sun drifted toward the west. It wouldn't be long before the days grew significantly shorter— and colder. Snow often fell at this latitude by mid-September. Sometimes sooner. But Eric's home was warm and cozy, and Laura pictured them curled up on the couch in front of the fireplace, protected and safe, while storms whipped around outside.

"You think we ought to get the twins a puppy?" he asked.

She slid him a surprised look. "Why don't we wait for a while? They'll appreciate a dog more when they're older, and I won't have to deal with diapers and housebreaking a puppy at the same time."

"Sounds reasonable. But they ought to have a big dog, not a poodle. You know, one of those breeds who have to grow into their feet."

"I assume that translates into you've always wanted a big dog for yourself?"

He shrugged sheepishly. "Blame it on a deprived childhood—at least until Oliver Oakes brought me here to the ranch. We always had a dog around then."

Her heart went out to him. His early childhood had been terrible, and she was sure he'd take care to see that the twins would have a better one. She vowed to do her part, too.

When they returned to the corral an hour or so later, Laura felt as though she'd been granted a special interlude that had brought her and Eric closer together. And when he made love to her that night, he seemed more tender, more loving than ever.

Her climax brought tears of joy, marred only by the realization that he still had not spoken the words of love she so desperately wanted to hear.

THE FOLLOWING DAY Eric came home for lunch. He did that as often as he could, and Laura found herself looking forward to his company. They'd talk about his work and whatever gossip he'd picked up around town. He'd spend a few minutes playing with the twins if they were awake.

She had just slid a plate in front of him at the kitchen table, a roast beef sandwich stacked high and a side of fruit and cottage cheese when she heard a car arriving out front.

She glanced out the window and her heart plummeted.

Russ Ungar hadn't given up his quest to claim the twins. He was back.

This time he'd brought a friend with him, a man wearing a dark suit and carrying a briefcase.

Chapter Thirteen

"Eric!"

At Laura's soft cry of alarm, Eric looked up from his sandwich. Her face had gone as white as a winter snowstorm, her eyes as wide as if she'd seen a ghost.

"What's wrong?"

"Ungar. He just drove up with a friend."

Eric cursed and shoved back from the table. "Take the twins upstairs. I'll handle Ungar."

"No matter what, don't let him have the twins."

She scooped Becky out of the playpen that was set up in a corner of the kitchen, and Eric handed Mandy to her.

"He won't take them anywhere."

Not unless Ungar had gotten a court order, which seemed unlikely without a hearing. Since they hadn't been notified of any proceedings, and Laura was still the twins' legal guardian, Eric figured they were safe for the moment. But out of a need to protect the twins, he retrieved his revolver from the safe and strapped on his holster before answering the knock on the front door.

He acknowledged Ungar with a nod.

"Afternoon, Sheriff." Ungar's sneering smile revealed one broken tooth and another that had gone gray with decay. "I brought along my attorney this time. Meet Henry Smedling."

The man in question whipped out a business card, which Eric took but didn't examine. Instead he sized up the attorney—frayed shirt collar, a tie spotted with residue from more than a few meals, a cheap knockoff watch. Not a big-time player in the legal world and very likely the only lawyer in the state who would agree to represent Ungar. If he was an attorney at all.

"Are you gonna let us in or make us cool our heels out here again?" Ungar asked.

"Why should I let you two losers in?"

"We have a proposition for you, Sheriff Oakes. And your wife, of course." The attorney's voice was so sniveling, a jury would vote against his client on general principles as soon as the lawyer finished his opening statements.

Eric lifted his brows. These two guys had to be up to something. He needed to know what.

Opening the door wider, he stood back. "Don't bother to sit down, gentlemen. You won't be staying long."

As he ushered them inside, Laura came downstairs.

"Well now, there's the little lady of the house," Ungar said. "You taking good care of my sweet little babies, honey buns?"

A muscle flexed in Eric's jaw. "*Mr.* Ungar brought

his attorney along this trip," he told Laura, introducing Smedling.

Her gaze darted to the stranger and back to Eric. "What do they want?"

"Mrs. Oakes," the attorney began, "we appreciate you've become attached to the twins. Who wouldn't? I'm sure they're a delight to you. However, my client's paternal rights supersede yours when it comes to—"

"We haven't seen any proof your client is the father of the twins," Eric pointed out.

Putting his briefcase on the coffee table, Smedling opened it and removed a sheet of paper. "I have here an affidavit from my client stating his relationship with Ms. Amy Thorne. It provides details of where they lived and for how long, their cohabitation and conjugal activities during the period in which Ms. Thorne became pregnant with the twins."

"I can hardly wait to read the details about that," Eric said derisively.

Ungar barked a laugh. "She was one hot mama, I'll tell you that!"

"You beat her, you...you scum!" Laura cried.

Gesturing for Laura to be quiet, Eric took the affidavit from the attorney. At a quick glance he realized the form didn't offer any evidence that would stand up in court in a paternity case.

"This is bull, gentlemen. What are you after?"

"As it happens, Sheriff Oakes," the smarmy attorney said, "my client is sympathetic to your situation and to your desire—and that of Mrs. Oakes—to raise the twins yourselves.''

''Then you can leave and never come back,'' Laura said, practically lunging toward to the door to let them out.

Eric gestured for her to be quiet. He intended to handle Ungar...in his own way.

Smedling continued. ''On the other hand, if Mr. Ungar were to give up all parental rights, it would cause him great mental suffering. These two precious little girls, who are the subject of our dispute, might be the only children he ever fathers. To never enjoy their affection and love would be a great loss to him.''

Eric was beginning to see a very clear picture emerging, and it looked like a scam to him.

''What sort of consideration are you looking for in order to ease his...mental anguish?''

''It is hard to set a dollar value on that kind of pain,'' the attorney countered self-righteously.

''How does ten thousand dollars sound?''

Ungar was quick to say, ''Make it twenty.''

''No deal.''

''Eric! If all it takes is money—''

''No deal, I said.'' What Eric needed was proof that Ungar wasn't the twins' father. Nothing less would free them of the man, no matter how much or how often they tried to pay him off.

Getting in his face, Ungar said, ''You'd better listen to your old lady, Sheriff.''

Laura grabbed Eric's arm.

''Trust me, Laura.'' He glanced away from Ungar

to meet her frantic gaze, hoping she'd believe he knew what he was doing. "We're not going to give this scumbag a dime. The twins are ours until a court says otherwise."

A snarl rose from Ungar's throat. "You know damn well if I get those babies away from her, there's no way in hell you're ever gonna get a piece of her again."

His crude remark would have been enough for Eric to punch Ungar under almost any circumstance. In this case he had an even better motive.

Bringing up his fist, he landed a direct hit to the bridge of Ungar's nose.

"Yeow!"

"Eric, what are you doing?"

Blood gushed from Ungar's nose, and he staggered backward.

Quickly Eric produced a clean handkerchief from his pocket. "Sorry about that," he said mildly.

Ungar pressed the handkerchief to his nose. "I'b gunna sue you, Oakes."

Shrugging, Eric said, "Could I help it if you were crowding my personal space when I reach up to swat a bug?"

Smedling took his client by the arm. "Come on, Russ. These people are being unreasonable. We'll see them in court."

"Please, Eric, don't let him leave this way," Laura pleaded. "Tell him you're sorry. Tell him we're willing to discuss his terms."

"Nope. The only thing I want from this guy is my handkerchief back."

Ungar tossed the blood-soaked square of cotton to the floor. Carefully Eric picked it up, then blocked Laura's way as she tried to follow the two men out the door.

"Are you sure you know what you're doing?" she asked, visibly shaken by the exchange.

"I hope so." Although, he had taken a risk and could end up in court on an assault charge—not an ideal situation for a sheriff. Still, based on his intuition, it had been worth the chance.

"He was going to sign over his paternity rights." Laura raced to the window to watch the pair leave. "I don't care how much money they wanted. I would give anything, the money from selling my condo—"

"And keep on giving year after year, if my guess is right."

She whirled. "What are you talking about?"

"He was trying to blackmail us. If we'd paid him off once, he would have come back for more, again and again. We'd never get rid of him."

"But now he'll take the children. I would rather—"

"I don't think he's their father."

She looked at him dumbfounded, then crossed the room to pick up the affidavit that he'd dropped on the coffee table. She scanned it quickly.

"How would he know all these details if he wasn't—"

"We're not even sure those details are accurate.

You said yourself you and your mother were out of touch with Amy. He could have made everything up. Or maybe someone else told him where Amy had been living.''

''Who?''

''I don't know.'' Taking her hand, he led her into the kitchen where he found a plastic Baggie and slipped his bloodied handkerchief inside, zipping it closed.

''What are you doing with that?''

Setting the Baggie on the counter, he took her by the shoulders, caressing her, trying to calm her. ''Listen to me. What's not in that affidavit, and what he didn't volunteer, is a blood test. That's the only way he can *prove* he is the twins' biological father.''

''Maybe he recognizes he isn't in a position to raise the twins as well as we could, and he's willing to give up his rights for that reason.''

''Plus twenty thousand dollars.'' She was so damn softhearted, she was willing to give the lowest of the low the benefit of the doubt. Eric wasn't. ''Trust me, Blue Eyes. I wouldn't willingly give up my own kids for a million bucks. Twenty million. So ask yourself why Ungar seems so eager.''

She hesitated, and he could see her good reason warring with her emotions. She wanted the twins at any price.

''Because he's lying,'' she finally said.

''That's what I'm counting on.''

''And if you're wrong?''

''We'll still have a lot of ways to battle him in the

courts, starting with him being an unfit father because he tried, in effect, to sell his kids to us."

She still looked skeptical but she nodded her head. "What do we do now?"

"Do you know the twins' blood type?"

She thought for a moment. "It's A. A-positive."

"That's pretty common but maybe we'll get lucky." He nodded toward the Baggie on the counter. "I'm going to take my handkerchief over to Kristi and Doc Justine at the clinic. We'll see if Ungar's blood type matches."

Her eyes widened. "That's why you hit him, isn't it?"

"Among other reasons." It had felt damn good, too. He didn't have patience with any man who physically *or* verbally abused a woman. Ungar had deserved what Eric had laid out.

"And if Ungar's blood is A-positive?"

His forehead tightened. "Then I'll ship the handkerchief off to the lab at Great Falls that does DNA testing. They'll be able to tell us if Ungar is the twins' father—or a fraud."

"How long will that take?"

"A few days. Meanwhile I'm still investigating, trying to find a connection between Ungar and Amy. Or Ungar and some other man Amy had been living with. That so-called affidavit he provided is going to give me some new leads to follow."

Crossing her arms, Laura hugged herself as though a winter wind had slipped in through an open window. "You do realize if you find someone else, the girls' real father—if it's not Ungar—you may create a bigger problem than we already have.''

Yeah, Eric knew that. But he didn't have much of a choice. He either had to prove Ungar wasn't the twins' father—or deal with the man the rest of the girls' lives. He wasn't about to do that voluntarily.

''All right. You're the cop. You must know what you're doing.''

Her words were slow and hesitant but they said that she trusted him. Under the circumstances, that was a lot.

Eric hoped to God she was right.

THE BELL ON THE CLINIC DOOR jingled as Eric stepped inside. He was greeted by the faint scent of antiseptic and a mother with her two children in the waiting room. Eric walked right on by them into Doc Justine's office area.

''You got an emergency, Sheriff?'' she asked. ''Or do you always bust in here without an appointment when folks are waiting?''

''I've got an emergency.'' He produced the Baggie with the bloody handkerchief. ''Have you got the equipment to determine blood type?''

Kristi appeared. ''Whose blood is it?''

''The guy who's trying to take the twins away from us. I'm hoping to prove he isn't their father.''

''You cut him?'' the doc asked.

''Punched him in the nose.''

''Wish I'd had the pleasure myself.'' Coming to her feet, Justine took the Baggie from him. ''Kristi, you do the Jamison boys' physicals. I'll see what we've got here.''

Kristi stopped Eric before he could follow the doctor. ''Is Laura all right?''

''She's upset, but she'll be fine if it turns out the guy doesn't have the same type blood as the twins.''

''I'll drop in later this afternoon, see how she's doing.''

''Thanks, Kristi. She'll appreciate it.''

She gave his arm a squeeze, then released him to find Justine in the back room she used as a lab. Fussing with her medical equipment, the doc was sitting on a stool in front of a microscope on the table.

She didn't look up when he arrived. ''It won't speed things up if you hover over my shoulder, you know.''

He stayed near the door. ''We're kind of anxious to know the answer.''

''I'll have to get a blood sample from the twins to compare.''

''They're A-positive.''

''So are about half the people in the country.''

''Then let's hope Ungar is in the minority.''

The seconds ticked by so slowly that each beat of the clock felt like an hour. If Ungar was any blood type besides A-positive, his gamble would pay off.

Eric couldn't stand still. He began to pace. Damn, what was taking so long?

Doc Justine spun around on the stool. ''Sorry. This blood is A-positive.''

Eric blew out a disappointed breath. ''Can you

package up the handkerchief for me? I'll have to take it to the lab in Great Falls.'' He could overnight express it via the postal service but it would be faster if he drove into town himself. He wanted answers as soon as possible, and he knew people who worked in the forensic lab.

"When Kristi's done with the Jamison boys I'll send her over to draw some blood from the babies. The lab will need to compare the samples.''

"Thanks.'' Doing an about-face, he marched out of the lab, past the display cases in the front hallway that held an array of antique medical equipment and out the front door.

He hated to think he'd guessed wrong about Ungar, hated even more the possibility that his half sister had been hooked up with a man like that. If only he'd known she existed, he could have taken care of her. Given her a home. Convinced her she deserved better than a lowlife like Ungar. Every woman did.

Worse, he didn't want Laura to feel as though she had misplaced her trust in him.

LAURA HAD WRAPPED Eric's mostly uneaten sandwich in plastic wrap, washed up the lunch dishes, scrubbed the kitchen sink and counter until they shone and was considering using her nervous energy to do the same to the floor when Eric returned.

"What happened?'' Her heart lodged in her throat at his worried expression.

He shook his head. "Life's never easy, is it? I'm going to have to drive to Great Falls.''

"Ungar has the same blood type?"

"Kristi's going to come over in a few minutes to draw blood from the twins for DNA comparison."

Laura covered her mouth with her hand to prevent herself from crying out. Her whole body trembled. The fear that she might lose the twins had never been so strong. She felt as though she was being torn asunder atom by atom.

Sensing her terror, Eric wrapped his arms around her. His khaki uniform shirt was smooth against her cheek, his body warm against the chill of dread that filled her heart.

"Don't fall apart on me now, Blue Eyes. Ungar isn't going to get the twins. I promised you, didn't I?"

"I'll go with you to Great Falls. We'll take the twins." She wanted to be with him, needed his reassurance.

"I'm going to drive there and straight back. No sense messing up the twins' schedule. I'll be home by bedtime."

She hated that he was being so logical when her emotions were in a turmoil, but she nodded her agreement. He knew what he was doing.

"I'll get Rory or Kristi to stay with you," he said.

"No, I'm fine. I'm keeping the doors locked." She wasn't fine, of course, but she couldn't allow Ungar to turn her into a frightened mouse.

He lifted her chin. "Have you ever used a pistol?"

"My father taught me to shoot, but it's been years

since I've—'' Her stomach knotted on a new fear. ''Why?''

''I don't think Ungar will show up while I'm gone, and he wasn't armed the other day when he came to call. Still, I'd feel better if I knew you could protect yourself and the twins.''

God, things seemed to be spiraling out of control. ''I think I remember enough to use a gun if I have to.''

His fingers slipped through her hair, and he tucked a few strands behind her ear. ''I'd like you to be a little better than that. I've got a short practice range in the barn that I use so I can keep qualified. After Kristi comes, I'm going to take you out there and give you a refresher course. I need to know you're safe with a loaded weapon.''

She couldn't argue with his reasoning. Her father had drilled gun safety into her. She would expect nothing less from Eric.

THE SHOOTING RANGE was twenty-five feet long, the target small and backed by piles of hay. The ten-shot semiautomatic pistol and ammunition clip Eric handed her, the extra weapon he kept in the kitchen safe, felt heavy in Laura's hand.

''You remember how to load the clip?'' he asked.

She nodded, never more aware of Eric's occupation and the danger it represented. She trembled a little as she slipped the clip into the grip, cocked the pistol and felt the first bullet slide into firing position. The scent of gun oil mixed with the elemental aromas in the barn and Eric's heady masculine scent. Everything about him spoke of rugged virility. And courage. Yet he was the same man who could gently cuddle a baby or love a woman with such tenderness it brought tears to her eyes.

She could not imagine loving any other man with the same depth of feeling that she loved Eric. Or wish more desperately that she could give him the sons he deserved.

"You okay?" he asked.

She blinked back a sheen of tears that blurred her vision. "You don't really think Ungar will come back, do you?"

"I think it's smart to be prepared."

She swallowed hard and took a deep breath. "I'm ready."

Standing behind her, his warm breath barely a caress across her neck, he lifted her right arm. "Use your left hand to steady your aim."

"You sure the bullet won't go through the back wall and hit one of your horses?"

"I'm sure. Besides, they're in the side corral."

"Good planning."

"Okay, line up on the target and squeeze—don't pull—the trigger."

It sounded like a cannon had gone off, and the gun jerked in her hand. Dust blew up from the bale of hay well above the still-unmarked target.

"Looks like I'm a little out of practice."

"You'll be fine. Just remember it's going to kick on you. Keep the nose down. Try it again."

She'd never been fond of guns or shooting even though her father wanted her to be familiar with using a weapon. Now that she might have to safeguard the twins from Ungar, she was well motivated.

Her second shot hit the target in line with the bull's-eye but several inches high. Her third try found the inner ring.

"Good. That one will slow a man down."

She shuddered. "I'm not sure I could actually squeeze the trigger with the pistol pointed at a person."

"I think you could, if that was the only way you could protect the twins."

Or protect you, she thought, knowing she'd do anything within her power to keep Eric out of harm's way, as well. She could only wonder if he felt the same way about her.

She finished the magazine clip and Eric took the pistol from her. Half the bullets had found the target if not the center of the rings.

He caught her under her chin. "You did good, Blue Eyes."

"It's scary to think I may actually have to use a gun on someone."

"Scary for me, too. But I want you to promise you'll mean business if you have to use that weapon. The worst thing that could happen is to have a perp take the gun away and use it on you."

"I know."

"I can count on you?"

She nodded, whispering, "Yes."

He lowered his head and found her mouth in a deep, searing kiss that sealed their bargain. Heat spiraled through her. Her blood roared through her veins. She moaned, instinctively reaching for him. Wanting more.

She nearly sobbed aloud when he broke the kiss.

"I've got to get the samples to Great Falls."

"I know." They were both breathing hard. "You'll come right home after you drop off the blood at the lab?"

His lips quirked ever so slightly. "That's a promise I won't have any trouble keeping."

In her heart of hearts, his eagerness thrilled her. "I'll wait up for you."

ERIC SPENT THE BETTER PART of the next day on the phone. He talked with the police chief in Helena, and even managed to reach the officer who had responded to a domestic dispute call at the address Ungar had listed on his so-called affidavit.

With a single call to the state bar association, he'd discovered Henry Smedling wasn't an attorney at all. The guy was no more than a jailhouse lawyer, who'd learned his way around a few law books while he'd been in prison himself for fraud. A sure sign Ungar's effort to claim paternity rights was nothing more than a poorly conceived con job.

But the most productive call he'd made was to the warden at the state prison.

By late afternoon when he locked up the sheriff's

office, he was feeling optimistic and impatient to share his latest theory about Ungar with Laura.

As he swung into his patrol car for the short drive home, he realized that before his marriage he'd never been in a hurry to go home. The empty house had held little appeal and no welcome.

Now when he walked in the door, more often than not there was the scent of something baking in the oven or cooking on the stovetop. There might be a vase of wildflowers in the middle of the kitchen table, collected while she took the twins for a stroller ride. She'd set out place mats and silverware, napkins.

In the rest of the house dust didn't pile up like it used to, though he didn't know how she found the time to clean and dust when she had to care for the twins. When he was doing the child care that's all he could manage, and then he seemed to be pulled in two different directions at once and desperately wished he had two sets of hands.

As easily as a duck takes to water, she'd turned his house into a home.

He'd never experienced that before. Not really. Sure, Oliver Oakes had been a damn good father in all the ways that mattered. But he'd had a hard edge to him, not soft and caring in the way Laura was with the twins.

And with him.

As he pulled the cruiser into the garage for the night, he realized no one had taught him anything about love. Except for the gut-wrenching love he felt for the twins, he'd never experienced anything but a temporary relationship with a woman. He'd been afraid to try, afraid in the long run a woman would find him lacking in some way—as his mother had.

He didn't want to be abandoned again so he didn't develop attachments. As easy as that.

But maybe he ought to reconsider his strategy.

Unlocking and walking in the back door, he tossed his hat on a peg in the mud room and strolled into the kitchen.

He sniffed the air. Chocolate-chip cookies! A plateful sat on the counter. He snatched one before strolling into the living room.

His breath caught in his lungs at the sight of Laura stretched out on the floor playing with Becky, lifting the infant over her head, bringing her closer to nuzzle her and pressing her up again. The baby loved it, her mouth wide open, giggling with excitement.

Maybe Laura, with all the love she had to give, was capable of teaching him to love, too.

Chapter Fourteen

"Looks like Becky may have a future as a gymnast."

Laura started at the sound of Eric's voice. She hadn't heard him come in and, as usual, her heart responded with a jolt of pleasure to have him home.

"I don't know," she said. "She gets such terrible giggles, we may be looking at a circus clown instead."

Sitting on the couch nearby, he extended his hands for the baby. "I think I'd rather have her be daddy's little-stay-at-home girl."

Laura passed Becky to him, smiling as he settled the baby in the crook of his arm like the experienced daddy he'd become. She rolled to her feet, wincing a little at a niggling pain in her side.

"I've got bad news for you, Eric. I intend to raise two independent young ladies who'll make their own decisions about their future."

He chuckled. "Maybe so, but they'll always come home to Daddy, won't you, Tinkerbell?" The baby blew a juicy bubble in response.

Home to both of us, Laura wanted to say but swallowed the words that would give away too much of her heart.

Picking up Mandy from her playpen, Laura sat down across from Eric, jiggling the baby on her knees. "Were you able to find out anything about Ungar today?"

"I was. And about his phony attorney, too."

"Phony?"

"As much a crook as Ungar, which lends a whole lot of credence to my theory their whole deal is a scam."

She exhaled in relief, brushing a quick kiss to Mandy's forehead. "Thank heavens. But what about Ungar?"

"For a time he had a cell mate named Christopher Barry. He was a young guy, not much older than Amy, with a big mouth and a violent temper. He got into a brawl a couple of months after he was sent to state prison. Somebody slipped a homemade shiv between his ribs."

Laura gasped. "Someone killed him?"

"Right. I'm thinking if this Christopher guy was Amy's boyfriend, he might have told Ungar about her. The details of their relationship. At least enough to fill in some blanks on that affidavit he gave us."

"So if he was their father, he's dead now. He'll never be a part of their lives?"

"That's what I'm thinking."

She ran her hand over the blond crown of Mandy's head. "I'm not sure how to react. It's terrible, in a way, that the girls will never know their father. But he was a violent man and a criminal. I can't feel badly that he'll never have any influence over them.''

"*If* I'm guessing right and Christopher Barry was their father. Not Ungar.''

"We may never know, will we?''

"Maybe it's better that way, for us and the girls.''

"Almost anything would be better than finding out Ungar is their biological father.'' Holding Mandy with one hand, she rubbed at her side again. She'd been achy all day, as though she was coming down with something. Her immune system was probably on the fritz due to too much stress in her life.

"I talked to the police in Helena, too, but there was no record of a domestic dispute call regarding Amy. I was hoping to get a description of the guy she was living with.''

"She probably never called the cops. Whomever it was had convinced her she deserved what she got.''

He grimaced and shook his head. "I wish I could return the favor.''

That was one of the many reasons Laura had fallen in love with Eric. He was protective of those he loved. Even though he'd never met his half sister, he'd automatically included Amy within the circle of those he felt obliged to defend.

"How soon will we hear on the DNA tests?'' she asked.

"The technician said he'd rush it.'' He shrugged as though he was unable to predict a time. "It may depend if he gets a rush order for a criminal trial or something.''

"I understand." Which didn't make the waiting any easier.

Deciding it was time to fix dinner, she passed Mandy to Eric. He was so comfortable with the twins, she had no qualms about letting him take over the parental duties with both babies.

In the kitchen, she got down a bottle of aspirin and swallowed a couple of pills. If she'd picked up a flu bug somewhere, she hoped she wouldn't give it to the twins.

Realizing she wasn't the least bit hungry, she forced herself to prepare a chicken breast, some squash and a baked potato for Eric. He could fill up on chocolate-chip cookies and canned peaches for dessert, if he wanted.

About the time she was ready to serve dinner, the sounds of fussing babies rose in volume, so she fixed two bottles, zapping them in the microwave. She'd feed the twins while Eric ate. Her uneasy stomach rebelled at the thought of food, anyway.

"Dinner," she called.

"Hope you've got something for these famished youngsters. The way they've been eating lately, neither one of them is going to fit into their prom dress." Juggling Mandy, he slipped Becky into her car seat. "Not that I'm going to let either of them date until they're thirty, of course."

Laura smiled but she couldn't find enough energy to laugh at his joke. Her face felt clammy and her stomach was threatening rebellion.

"Eric, I don't think I should—"

The phone rang. She rolled her eyes. Just once she'd like to have dinner without crying babies or Eric being called out on the job.

He got the phone while she got the bottles out of the microwave. To quiet Mandy, she propped her bottle then fetched Becky from Eric's arms. He wasn't talking. Just listening intently. Laura hoped it wasn't an emergency, because she was going to have to go to bed early. So far the aspirin hadn't done much.

Sitting down at the table, and trying not to breathe on Becky, she slipped the bottle into the baby's eager mouth. Despite feeling miserable, she couldn't stop the smile that curved her lips or the feeling of maternal love that welled up in her. She'd never be so sick that the emotional high the twins gave her would vanish.

Eric touched her shoulder. An emphatic smile lit up his face, and his pale blue eyes glistened. "We're home free, Laura."

She cocked her head in question.

"That was the guy from the lab. Ungar's blood doesn't match the twins. He's not their father."

Her eyes fluttered closed and her shoulders sagged in relief. "Thank God!"

"Man, I'd really like to get my hands around Ungar's throat for the worry he put us through. That phony attorney, too. All they wanted was money. They both ought to be locked up, and I'd personally be willing to throw away the key."

"Eric!" She thrust the baby into his arms. "I've

got to—'' Hand over her mouth, she raced for the bathroom.

Startled, Eric tightened his grip on the baby and grabbed for the bottle before it dropped to the floor. "What's wrong?"

He hadn't expected Laura to react to such good news by bolting from the room. He'd been thinking of a celebratory kiss. A good long smooch followed by an even more interesting activity after the twins went down for the evening.

He'd been dead wrong.

With a quick glance at Becky to see that she was okay on her own, he carried Mandy to the downstairs bathroom where Laura had disappeared. During the past couple of days, he'd realized he could finally tell the twins apart—the shape of their brows, the different sounds of their cries and mostly their personalities.

He rapped his knuckles lightly on the bathroom door. "You okay?"

Her moan sounded miserable.

Hesitating only a moment, he shoved the door open. She was sitting on the floor, her arm draped over the commode, and she looked as sick as a dog. A panicky fist gripped him in the chest.

"Laura, honey, what's wrong?"

She shook her head. Her hair looked lank, her forehead damp with sweat. "Flu, I think."

"What can I get you?"

She tried to wave him off. "The twins, you take care of—"

"I will. But I can't leave you here like this."

"Just go. Go. I'll be fine."

She wasn't fine, and he was helpless to know what to do. Dammit, he'd dragged broken, bloodied bodies out of crumpled cars. Rescued people who'd been stranded on a cliff three hundred feet high. Pulled people out of fiery buildings.

But he'd never felt like this. Powerless to help the woman he'd come to care about, and more than a little bit concerned.

From the other room he heard Becky cry.

"I'll be back," he promised, edging reluctantly out of the bathroom. Laura looked so weak, she could barely lift her head. "Should I call Doc Justine?"

"No." She waved him away again. "Babies."

"Right." He hurried to Becky, determined to get the twins fed and down as soon as possible. Then he'd see to Laura.

Maybe it was just a bad case of the flu, he told himself. Nothing anyone could do about that. A cold cloth on her forehead. Broth when she was feeling better. Lots of liquids, he remembered as he patted Becky's back and brought up a giant-size burp, making her feel instantly better. No need to panic.

Laura screamed.

Frantic, Eric managed to get both babies into the living room and in the playpen, giving them a quick, "Your mom needs me," before hustling to Laura in the bathroom.

"What's happening?"

Holding her belly, she was practically rolling on

the floor. "It hurts. Oh, damn, it hurts! I'm sorry." She groaned in an apparent effort not to scream again. Her face was as white as bone, her lips twisted into a grimace.

That didn't look like flu to him. "I'm calling the doctor."

His fingers shook as he punched in the phone number. It took three rings before Kristi answered.

As coherently as possible, Eric told her what was going on.

"Can you bring her over here?" Kristi asked.

"The twins. I can't—"

"We'll both be right there," Doc Justine said on the clinic's extension phone.

Barely hanging up and without saying goodbye he raced back to the bathroom. He sat on the floor and cradled Laura's head in his lap. Sweat poured off her forehead, her cheeks were flushed. Grabbing a silly little fringed guest towel from the rack above him, something Laura had brought with her from Helena, he wiped away the dampness from her face.

"It's okay, sweetheart. Doc's coming. Kristi, too. They'll know what to do."

"I feel like such a wimp. It's got to be just a bad case of the—"

"Naw. Think of this as an exercise to make me feel like a hero."

"You are, you know." Her whole body shuddered in his arms. "A hero."

God, what was taking the doc so long? The damn

clinic was only a block away. By now they could have driven to Great Falls and back.

One of the twins started to fuss again. But Eric wasn't going to leave Laura. Not now. Both babies were safe. He'd seen to that. Laura wasn't.

"That's Becky," she whispered hoarsely. "She can be so fussy—"

"She's fine. The doc will be here soon. Then I'll see to her." It figured Laura would be worried about her baby instead of focusing on her own pain. Whatever heroics he'd ever managed in his entire life paled in comparison to her maternal instincts. "Try to relax," he urged her.

Distress shadowed her beautiful eyes and etched lines of tension across her face. "If anything happens to me—"

"Shh, nothing's going to happen. You've got a nasty bug of some sort. Doc will give you a magic shot that will hurt like hell and you'll be fine. You'll see."

She didn't look convinced, but by now he'd heard the local medical team arrive. The crying baby hushed a moment before Doc Justine squeezed her way into the bathroom.

"Okay, young man, let me take a look. You go see to your babies."

Doc virtually shouldered Eric aside. He had no choice but to leave the room. Among other things, there wasn't enough space for three adults to fit in the guest bathroom.

Feeling drained and weak in the knees, he staggered out of the bathroom to find Kristi and the twins. She seemed to have the babies under control.

"You look awful, Eric. Sit down." She gestured toward the couch.

He sat as ordered. "Laura's real sick. I don't think it's the flu."

"Justine will know what's wrong."

God, he hoped so. Leaning over, he buried his face in his hands. What would he do if he lost Laura? It would be like the sun not coming up in the morning, spring not following winter.

"Eric!" Doc called.

He sprang up from the couch, racing back to the bathroom. "What?"

"I want you to carry Laura into the living room, put her on the couch. I can't examine her properly here."

Ignoring Laura's protest that she could walk, the doc moved out of the way and Eric picked up his wife in his arms. The moan she stifled against his chest nearly drove him to his knees. She was hurting, and it was something he couldn't fix.

Once he had Laura on the couch, the doc poked and prodded at her abdomen, more times than not drawing a cry or wince from Laura.

The examination didn't take long. Doc Justine sat on the edge of the coffee table keeping an eye on her patient.

"We could do a blood test," she said, "but it's not likely to change my diagnosis. Laura, you've got an acute case of appendicitis. You need to get to a hospital right away.''

"But the twins—"

"You don't have any choice," Doc insisted. "If your appendix ruptures—and it may—you'll be in worse trouble than you are now.''

Forcing himself to stay calm, to handle the emergency, Eric said, "I'll put in a call to the medi-vac helicopter in Great Falls.''

"It'd be faster to drive her yourself," Doc said. "The weather's good, the roads clear. The helicopter would take almost as long to get up in the air and here as it would for you to do the trip yourself with your lights flashing.''

"Okay. Sounds good.'' Hell, nothing sounded good when Laura was in danger of a ruptured appendix.

Kristi said, "One of us should go with them.''

"You know," the doc said with a wink, "I've been itching to get my hands on those twins to give 'em a good cuddle.'' She glanced at Kristi. "You're more agile than I am these days and can pretty well do anything I could do. Hustle on back to the clinic, get an IV set to go. While you folks are off to Great Falls, I'll indulge my grandmotherly instincts and give those twins lots of lovin'.'' Taking Laura's hand, she gave her an encouraging smile. "If that's okay with you.''

"At this point, I'm not exactly prepared to argue with anything you say. Just take care of—''

"They'll be fine," Justine assured her. "And so will you.''

Kristi said, "I'll be back in under five minutes. I'll let Rory know I'm going with you."

Eric wasn't quite as confident as Doc Justine as he readied the SUV cruiser to act as an ambulance. He was supposed to be strong; the thought of losing Laura made him weak. Never before had he known this feeling of sheer terror.

He could only hope he'd be able to hold himself together, keep his emotions under control, until he got Laura safely to the hospital.

HE'D ALERTED THE HOSPITAL that he was bringing in a patient, and he'd driven as if he was on an Indy racecourse, lights flashing, siren wailing. Even so, it seemed like an eternity before he whipped his police cruiser up to the hospital Emergency entrance and brought it to a halt.

He bolted from the car just as a couple of orderlies with a gurney and a nurse appeared. With a quick, professional summary, Kristi brought them up-to-date on Laura's pulse, blood pressure and the pain medication she'd been given. The hospital staff placed Laura on the gurney.

Eric held her hand as she was wheeled inside.

She looked up at him with a sleepy smile. "That was some wild ride, Sheriff."

"I wanted to get you here in a hurry."

"You did fine. I knew you would."

Her words filled him with an unexpected sense of awe. She'd trusted him to get her safely to the hospital—just as she'd trusted him to be the father of the twins she dearly loved. And to be her husband, in sickness and in health, until death do them part.

Emotion clogged his throat. *Don't die, Blue Eyes. Please.*

''We've got her, Sheriff,'' the nurse said as a doctor arrived to examine Laura. ''You can wait in the lobby. We'll keep you posted.''

He couldn't seem to let go of her hand.

She gently squeezed his fingers. ''I'll be fine, Eric. Let the doctor do her work.''

Nodding, he bent down and brushed a kiss to her lips. ''I'll be right outside if you need me.''

''I know,'' she whispered.

Kristi took his arm, gesturing that they should leave the examination room. He still didn't want to go, but he didn't have much choice.

In the lobby, a half-dozen people were waiting in various stages of boredom and anxiety, watching the flicker of a TV set mounted on a faux marble post.

Kristi said, ''You go move your cruiser away from the emergency entrance, then check at the admissions desk. I'll wait right here. If anything happens, I'll be able to keep you posted.''

''Right.'' Feeling muddled, as though he'd been the one getting a heavy dose of painkiller, Eric followed Kristi's instructions.

At the admissions desk, he discovered he didn't know Laura's social security number or her date of birth, which she must have listed on their marriage certificate but he hadn't been paying attention. Or if she had any allergies, though she hadn't mentioned any. She would have told him about that, he was sure. Well, mostly sure.

Damn it! Laura was his wife and there was so much he didn't know about her. She liked flowers because she was always picking a few wildflowers and putting them in a vase on the kitchen table. She could cook and bake like a whiz, and probably knew more about history than he'd ever wanted to know. And she had a tiny mole on the side of her neck that he loved to kiss.

But he didn't know her favorite color or what kind of music she liked. Where she liked to go on vacation. If she hated going to the dentist as much as he did.

By the time he finished with the admissions clerk, he was mentally kicking himself around the block. *Don't die, Laura. There's a lot I want to learn about you yet. It may take me years to get all the answers.*

Kristi stood when he returned to the lobby. "They took her up to surgery a couple of minutes ago."

A painful, hollow sensation filled his stomach. "I should have been here. Gone with her."

"They'd already given her a light anesthetic. She was sleeping when they took her up." She placed a reassuring hand on Eric's arm. "We can wait upstairs, if you'd like."

"Maybe we should call her mother," he suggested. "Let her know what's happening. Information probably has her number."

"I'll take care of it after I get you settled. I'd just as soon not have a big guy like you pass out on me. You're looking a little green around the gills."

Eric couldn't argue with her judgment. He felt as bad as if he were the one about to have surgery.

The upstairs waiting room was small and unoccupied at the moment, which left Eric alone with his thoughts while Kristi made the call to Laura's mom.

He sat on a narrow couch, elbows on his knees, head in his hands, picturing Laura, willing her to be okay. He never should have put her in the bind of *having* to marry him in order to be the twins' mom. That hadn't been fair. She'd had her life all planned out. Her teaching. Her curriculum job.

Then he'd turned stubborn and selfish, not wanting to give up the twins himself.

Kristi joined him on the couch. "Her mom's going to drive over. She'll be here as soon as she can."

"Thanks for making the call." He sure as hell was in no shape to hold a coherent conversation with Laura's mother or anyone else.

"I certainly hope Laura knows how much you love her."

Slowly he turned his head to look at Kristi. The lamplight haloed her reddish-gold hair.

"A guy like me? I'm not exactly capable of love."

"What makes you say a thing like that?"

"You know something about my background. Dumped by my mother when I was—"

"You love your brothers, don't you? Rory and Walker?"

"Well, yeah, but that's—"

"How about the twins? You worked so hard to

keep them, to be their dad, you must love them as much as I love Adam.''

''They're babies. My only living blood relatives. Sure I love 'em.'' What the hell was Kristi getting at?

''And yet you're out here, dying a thousand deaths yourself because Laura's having a relatively routine surgery, and you're trying to tell me you don't love her? Give me a break, White Eyes. You Oakes boys have to be as dumb as dirt when it comes to women and your emotions.'' She rolled her eyes in exasperation. ''Rory was exactly the same way with me.''

Eric stared at her for a long minute. *He loved Laura?* Rolling the idea around in his brain, he decided it fit. It fit comfortably, in fact. He wondered how long the thought had been hiding somewhere in the cracks and crannies of his brain without him being aware it was there.

He loved Laura. Somehow when he wasn't paying attention, he'd actually fallen in love with her—despite his background and his fear of not having the capacity to love a woman.

He grinned. *Well, I'll be damned!*

''I get the feeling a lightbulb just went on in that male brain of yours.''

''Yeah, it did.'' His smile broadened.

''Then I suggest you share your new insight with Laura at your earliest opportunity.''

''I'll do that.'' He swallowed hard as he had a second thought. Given that they had married for the sake of the twins, he wasn't all that sure how she would react to the news that he loved her. She might prefer to keep things as they were—a marriage that didn't carry a lot of emotional baggage.

Maybe *she* didn't love him.

What the hell! Not only didn't he know Laura's favorite color, he didn't know how she felt about him.

"Maybe I'd better hold off on telling her until she's feeling better," he muttered.

"Eric Oakes, if you love a woman you *have* to tell her. Anything else is cruel and unusual punishment, for heaven's sake."

He blinked again, recalling a conversation he'd had with Rory not that many months ago. His brother had been afraid to tell Kristi how he felt about her, and it almost cost him the woman he loved.

God, now he knew why Rory had been so scared. He was sweating bullets.

Patting his shoulder, Kristi said, "Tell her, Eric. I promise she loves you back. It's in her eyes every time she looks at you."

Chapter Fifteen

Eric picked up Laura's hand, curling her fingers over his palm. "How you doing, Blue Eyes?"

A lazy smile curved her lips. "A little woozy still, but I'm okay."

"Yeah, you're more than okay. The doctor said the surgery went perfectly. You'll be home in a day or two, and then I'm suppose to pamper you."

"That sounds nice. Remind me to thank the doctor for suggesting that."

"She didn't need to. I'd already figured that part out." He smoothed back a few damp strands of hair from her forehead. "I brought you flowers, too. From the gift shop downstairs."

She glanced toward the end of the bed where he'd placed the floral arrangement on the nightstand. "They're beautiful. I love daisies and chrysanthemums. They always look so cheerful."

"I'll keep that in mind for future reference." He'd keep her in flowers, too, for the rest of her life, if she'd let him.

"Where's Kristi?" she asked.

"Waiting outside. She wanted to give us some time alone. She also called your mom. She's on her way here, by the way."

Laura nodded. "She'll be worried."

"She'll be okay once she finds out that you came through surgery with flying colors." Taking a deep breath, he said, "There's something else I've figured out, besides the pampering part the doctor recommended."

"What's that?"

He tried to lick the dryness from his lips without much success. "I was so scared when you got sick, and then during that miserably long drive into town. And again when they took you into surgery. I was afraid I was going to lose you, Laura."

She looked surprised by his admission. "You didn't have to worry. I knew I was in good hands."

"The thing is…I hadn't realized…"

A tiny frown stitched its way across her forehead, and her eyes cleared with concern. "What's wrong, Eric? Tell me."

"Nothing's wrong, exactly. It's just that I…I love you, Laura. I don't know when it happened or quite how, but it did. And the thing is, I don't think I'm ever going to stop loving you."

She brought the back of his hand up to her face, rubbing it across her soft cheek as she smiled. "How nice…"

"I know I practically forced you to marry me so you could be a mom to the twins. I'd understand if you decide you don't want to stay married to me. I wouldn't even fight you for their custody, if that's what you want. They need you.''

Laura strained to break through the residual fog of anesthetic to understand what Eric was telling her. Hadn't he just said the words she'd longed to hear— that he loved her. And now he was giving her custody of the twins? ''Don't they need you, too?''

''Seems to me that mothers are extraimportant.''

''So are fathers. Amy wanted her babies to have both a mother and father. That's what you and I wanted, too.''

''Yeah, well, I thought maybe if I gave you a choice—''

''That I'd choose to stay with you?''

Looking more uncertain than she'd ever seen him, Eric glanced away. ''Something like that,'' he said.

Her old worry resurfaced, and she trembled on the inside. ''Even though I can't give you children of your own?''

''You and the twins are all I could ever want. If you decide to stay with me, later on—if it seems like a good idea—we could talk about adopting another kid or two. I mean, that's worked out pretty well for Walker—if you'd be willing.''

''I think I would.'' She'd been afraid no man would ever consider that option, that he would reject her because of her inability to bear the children he deserved. ''In which case, I have this really good idea. You do love me?'' His quick nod of agreement thrilled her. ''And I love you.''

He brightened. ''You do?''

"With all of my heart. Which is why it makes a lot of sense to me that we stay married for the next fifty years or so, raise the twins together, add a few more babies along the way however we can and maybe even bounce a few grandchildren on our respective knees before we're too old and creaky to enjoy them."

"Oh, God…" Without letting go of her hand, he dragged a chair closer and sat down heavily. "Grandchildren, huh?"

"When the girls are ready to start their own families."

"It better not be too soon," he said sternly. "I mean, teenage boys can be pretty—"

She laughed, which pulled the muscles in her abdomen, and tears of happiness filled her eyes.

He was instantly on his feet again. "What's happening? Are you hurting? I'll call the doctor."

"No. Just tell me again that you love me."

"I do." Bending over, he brushed a sweet kiss to her lips. "I love you, Laura Oakes. I always will."

She smiled, and tears squeezed out of the corners of her eyes. "I love you, my beloved husband. I'll love you forever, until death do us part." This time she knew the vows they were sharing came from two hearts that had found each other and their new promise was meant to last a lifetime.

A light rap on the door preceded her mother's appearance. "I'm sorry to interrupt, but I was worried. I came as soon as—"

"Come in, Mrs. Cavendish." Giving Laura's hand

a quick squeeze, Eric stepped away from the bed. "Your daughter's fine. In fact, we're both fine."

Without hesitation, Barbara Cavendish gave Laura a gentle hug and was quickly reassured that all was well, or would be soon. Kristi came into the room to add her own best wishes for a swift recovery.

Laura was feeling quite overwhelmed by all the attention—and the depth of love she saw in Eric's eyes—when her mother pulled an envelope from her purse.

"Bill Williams—our family attorney," she noted for Eric's and Kristi's benefit, "dropped by the other day. It seems Amy left a letter in his care at the time she was making plans for the twins if she should—" She halted, her chin quivering slightly.

"It's okay, Mom. We understand how much you loved Amy."

Barbara steadied herself. "Apparently Amy wanted you to have this letter on the twins' first birthday. But since Bill is retiring at the end of the month, he wanted to pass it on to you now so that it wouldn't be lost in the changeover at his law firm." She handed Laura the envelope with the attorney's return address.

"Do you want me to open it now?"

"I think so," her mother said.

Laura glanced at Eric, who gave her a shrug that said, "Your choice."

Opening the envelope, she unfolded a single sheet of paper covered with Amy's almost childish scrawl. Slowly she read her foster sister's last message.

Dearest Laura,

No one could have had a better sister than you were to me—or a better mother than Barbara was. If I disappointed you, I am sorry and wish I could have been a better person. I hope my babies, who I love with all my heart, will make it up to you by giving you all the love you deserve.

I know you think it strange that I insisted you try to locate my half brother. But you see, ever since I learned of his existence I've had this dream that you and Eric, wherever he is, would raise my babies together. Without knowing a thing about him, I'm hoping he'll be the kind of man who could love you and be kind to you, as a man should.

Forgive me if this was a silly dream. If it didn't work out as I had hoped, forgive me for trying to play matchmaker from the grave.

I love you and will be watching over you and the twins.

Amy

Laura's hand trembled, and she couldn't stop the flow of tears that ran down her cheeks.

Concerned, Eric took the letter from her nerveless fingers. "What is it?"

"It's perfect. Your sister sent me to find you because—"

She couldn't finish the thought, the swell of love she felt for Amy filled her throat and made her chest ache.

Eric scanned the letter. "I'll be darned," he said, passing it to Barbara, who let Kristi read it over her shoulder. There were tears shining in his eyes, too.

"She got her last wish," Laura whispered.

"Yeah, she did."

He bent over the bed railing to kiss her again, and Laura knew that somewhere Amy was looking down on them, smiling through her own veil of tears.

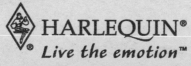

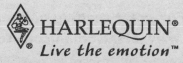

If you enjoyed what you just read,
then we've got an offer you can't resist!

Take 2 bestselling
love stories FREE!
Plus get a FREE surprise gift!

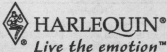